KT-362-845

MARGARET MOUNSDON

# THE EIGHTH CHILD

Complete and Unabridged

LINFORD
Leicester

First published in Great Britain in 2018

First Linford Edition
published 2019

A catalogue record for this book is available
from the British Library.

ISBN 978–1–4448–4228–9

Published by
F. A. Thorpe (Publishing)
Anstey, Leicestershire

Set by Words & Graphics Ltd.
Anstey, Leicestershire
Printed and bound in Great Britain by
T. J. International Ltd., Padstow, Cornwall

This book is printed on acid-free paper

# THE EIGHTH CHILD

Why is Posy Palmer the only one to be concerned when her old school friend, Iris Laxton, disappears? But as Posy begins to delve into Iris's past, she realises how little she really knew about her. When Posy's bicycle tyre is deliberately punctured, and evidence begins to disappear, the only person she can turn to for help is Sam Barrington, the charismatic ex-policeman who accused her of wasting police time when she reported another missing person six months previously. Will he believe her this time?

# Uncomfortable Reunion

'What are you doing here?' Sam Barrington demanded.

'Ms Palmer is concerned about her friend.' The eager smile on the hotel receptionist's face made Posy feel sick.

'And the friend is?' he enquired.

'One of our guests.'

The receptionist fluttered her eyelashes at Sam, obviously too well trained to betray the surprise she must be feeling at his brusque line of questioning.

Posy's flush deepened.

'Iris Laxton is staying in the Roberts Suite,' the receptionist explained. 'Ms Palmer was to have tea with her friend but the lady isn't in the lounge and we are unable to find her. Shall I page her?'

'Has Ms Palmer reported her missing, by any chance?' Sam asked in a reasonable voice.

Posy decided it was time she spoke up.

'I haven't gone quite that far yet.'

It was all Posy could do to stop her upper lip curling. Sam Barrington was an unfeeling brute and this knowledge came from personal experience.

'Leave this with me, Gaia,' Sam said. His smile had the desired effect on the receptionist.

A slight pressure on her elbow made Posy realise she was being ushered away from the reception desk and back into the lounge she had recently vacated.

'Shall we sit down here?' The tone of Sam's question meant refusal wasn't an option.

Posy sat down and waited for Sam to speak.

'Would you like some tea?' he enquired.

Posy, who had been looking forward to one of the Palace Hotel's famed cream teas, was tempted to refuse, but a hungry growl from her stomach let her down. He raised a hand and one of the hovering waitresses was by his side in an instant.

Moments later, a plate of scones accompanied by a luscious serving of blackcurrant jam and a generous amount of cream was placed in front of Posy, together with a selection of delicate finger sandwiches and the minuscule strawberry tarts that were the chef's speciality.

'Why don't I pour while you get going on that lot?' Sam picked up one of the teapots. 'Peppermint tea, wasn't it?'

Surprised he should have remembered her particular choice of tea, Posy nodded.

'Perhaps we should wait for Iris,' she stalled.

'I'm sure your friend will turn up — eventually,' Sam replied.

Posy ignored his jibe and took a warm scone off the plate.

If it hadn't been for Sam's presence, Posy would have enjoyed the experience of afternoon tea at the Palace. Sun streamed through the windows. Visitors to Sealbourne were taking advantage of the warm September sun to enjoy a stroll along the seafront.

All around her, Posy could hear the chink of teacups and the murmur of polite conversation. A piano tinkled in the background. It was the picture of gentility.

'Finished?' Sam enquired when only two sandwiches remained on the cake stand. 'Or do you think you could manage the last strawberry tart?'

Posy dabbed at her lips with the starched napkin provided.

'I left it for you. You look as though you could do with a sugar fix,' she replied with what she hoped was a sweet smile.

Posy wasn't sure but she thought she detected a slight softening of the expression on Sam's face. He glanced at his watch.

'I trust I'm not keeping you?' she felt compelled to ask.

'What time were you due to meet your friend?'

'Three o'clock.'

'It's now half past four.' Sam looked thoughtful. 'Is there any chance you may have got the wrong day?'

'Tuesday afternoon was the only time I could manage.'

'Indeed.'

'Anyway,' she added, refusing to respond to the doubt in his voice, 'what are you doing here? Shouldn't you be out somewhere apprehending villains who've strayed over the speed limit?'

'Is that how you break the law?' Sam's smile was deceptively innocent.

'I don't drive.' Posy felt immensely superior. 'Nice try,' she added, 'but you won't catch me breaking the law again.'

'I won't be catching anyone breaking the law again.'

'Really?' Posy refused to sound curious.

'I am no longer a member of the police force. I now work here. I'm head of security.'

'And you don't believe a word I said about Iris, do you?'

'Let's say I'm keeping an open mind on the matter.'

'I don't make a habit of reporting missing persons.'

'Don't you?'

The clotted cream churned in Posy's stomach.

Six months earlier she and Barry Grey had been part of a group protesting against proposed local development plans. They had been based outside the headquarters of a global investigative engineering corporation situated on the outskirts of Sealbourne.

One morning Barry had offered to fetch some supplies but had not returned. Posy had been deputised to report his disappearance to the police.

The interviewing officer had been Sam Barrington.

Posy had been taken into a side room to make a full statement. In her absence the protest group was moved on by the authorities and with a sense of outrage

Posy had gone back to the police to find out what they were doing to trace Barry.

Sam had again been on duty and had assured her everything possible was being done.

'This is because he's an activist, isn't it?' Posy had demanded.

'Not at all,' Sam had hastened to reassure her. 'Statistics show that many of the people who go missing do so because they want to.'

'Statistics prove nothing.'

'I think you'll find they do,' he assured her.

'Do you know bumblebees can't fly?'

'I beg your pardon?' Sam looked confused.

'It's been statistically proven that the body weight ratio doesn't work, but nobody seems to have informed the bumblebee.' Posy crossed her arms and waited for his reaction.

'Yes, well, that's all very interesting.' The expression in his world-weary eyes belied his words. 'But we seem to have strayed from the point.'

'So what are you going to do? Where is Barry? And don't tell me your resources are stretched. There were enough resources to disband our peaceful protest but not, it would seem, to find a missing person.

'Don't you care that he could be lying face down in a ditch, or worse?' Posy was breathing heavily as she finished speaking.

The interview room telephone gave a shrill ring. Sam picked it up with a look of relief.

'Barrington.'

Outside Posy could hear raised voices.

Sam finished his call and replaced the receiver.

'Tell me, Ms . . . ' he glanced at his notes, 'Palmer.'

'You're even having difficulty remembering my name, aren't you?'

'Were you and Mr Grey close friends?'

'Something's happened to him, hasn't

it? I knew it. This is your fault, if you'd done something earlier . . . '

'Just answer my question, please,' Sam snapped.

'Yes, we were friends. Does that satisfy you?'

'Close friends?'

'Yes, I suppose we were close.'

Posy saw no reason to go into the full details of their relationship. Barry disliked the term boyfriend and he found the word commitment equally restricting.

Sam shuffled the papers on the desk.

'I have some news for you, Ms Palmer. Perhaps you'd care to follow me.'

'Where are we going?'

Posy's heart was in her mouth as Sam opened the interview room door and stood to one side. The expression in his eyes was a mixture of sympathy and a deeper emotion that Posy couldn't put her finger on.

Surely they weren't going to ask her to identify a body?

9

A group of people were standing around the main desk. They parted at the sound of Posy's voice.

Standing in the middle of the group with an awkward smile on his face was Barry. Posy would have sagged against the wall if Sam hadn't supported her.

'Barry, where have you been?' Barry backed away as Posy shook off Sam's restraining arm.

Sam held Posy back.

At that moment a disturbance drew everyone's attention to the main door. A blonde entered, strolled over to Barry's side and linked her arm through his. She was wearing a powder-blue outfit more suited to a garden party than a police station.

'You wouldn't believe the trouble I had parking, darling,' she said in a husky voice. She fixed her eyes on the desk sergeant. 'I hear you've been looking for Barry.'

'That's right, miss,' the sergeant replied. 'He's been reported missing by that young lady over there.'

Still clinging on to Barry, the girl ignored Posy.

'It's madam, actually, not miss, and the reason Barry went missing was because we . . . ' She cast a coy glance in his direction. 'Shall I tell them, or do you want to do the honours, darling?'

'What she's trying to say is that we're married.' Barry avoided looking at Posy. 'This lady is my wife, Celeste.'

Celeste flashed her solitaire diamond under the police sergeant's nose.

'I'm sorry we caused a fuss but you see we had to get married in secret because Daddy wouldn't have approved of Barry's activist activities.

'Luckily, I talked him round and he's just treated us to lunch at the Palace Hotel. Wasn't that sweet of him?'

Posy hoped never to relive the humiliating scene that followed. She had been accused of wasting police time and in retaliation she had told Sam Barrington what she thought of modern policing methods before storming out of the station, hoping never to see him again.

Yet, less than six months later, she found herself in exactly the same position — another friend was missing, only this time nothing on earth was going to persuade her to go anywhere near the police.

'How much do I owe you for the tea?' Posy asked, unzipping her bag.

'Tea was on the house, with the compliments of the Palace Hotel,' Sam replied.

'In that case . . . ' Posy stood up. 'Thank you for your hospitality.'

'What about your friend?'

It annoyed Posy to have to crane her neck to look up to Sam who was now standing in front of her.

'I'm sure she'll contact me — eventually. But now, if you'll excuse me, I need to get on.'

'You'd better give me your details in case Ms Laxton reappears.'

'Do you take the name and address

of everyone who comes into this hotel?'

'I like to think our security remains at the highest level.'

Something in Sam's eyes told her this was one battle she wasn't going to win.

'Zephyr Cottage, Fisherman's Courtyard,' she mumbled.

Sam scribbled the details on a scrap of paper.

'Thank you.'

The concierge opened the lounge door for her with a polite bow.

Determined to keep her dignity, Posy swept out through the revolving front doors, down the steps and on to the promenade.

She swallowed the rising lump of concern blocking her throat.

'There's something I need to talk to you about, Posy.' Iris had sounded more than anxious during their brief telephone call. 'I know it's been ages since we've seen each other, but you won't let me down, will you?'

Posy cast a quick look up and down the promenade as if hoping Iris would suddenly appear and explain with her cheerful smile that one of them had got the time or date wrong, but there was no sign of her.

Posy hefted her bag higher on to her shoulder and began walking home.

If she wanted to find Iris she was on her own.

# Looking for Clues

Posy threw her paint-streaked cloth across the table in frustration. Jena stirred in her basket, sensing her mistress's mood.

'Come on.' Posy unhooked Jena's lead off its hook. 'We both need exercise.'

With an excited bark, Jena followed her downstairs.

As she was clipping Jena's lead to her collar there was a loud roar of an exhaust and a bright red convertible flashed into Fisherman's Courtyard.

The roof was down and the driver greeted them with a cheerful wave. Jena's tail went into overdrive and she strained her lead at the sight of the new arrival.

'Milo!' Posy straightened up in delight. 'I thought you were in Singapore.'

'I should have been but there was a crewing mix-up. We tossed a coin and I lost.' He eased his long legs out of the cramped seating space.

'And because you had nothing else to do, you decided to visit your big sister?'

'I wasn't going to hang around the flat all weekend.' Milo leaned over the steering wheel to retrieve his flight bag. 'Where are you going?' He nodded to her waterproof and walking shoes.

'I'm taking Jena for a walk along the beach.'

'Give me five to change and I'll join you.'

Posy sat down on the wooden bench outside to wait for Milo. Although they led separate lives she and her brother possessed that special closeness twins often enjoy.

As children they had relied on each other more than most siblings, with their father away on frequent lecture tours and their mother heavily involved in her charity work.

The older by ten minutes, Posy enjoyed bossing Milo. He was one of those people who took everything life threw at him with characteristic good humour but he was hopelessly disorganised.

She had a suspicion that the Singapore crewing mix-up was probably his fault.

'All set?'

He had done a quick change into navy blue sweater, jeans and deck shoes.

'I wish you'd let me sew those up for you.' Posy pointed to where his knee was sticking through a large gap in the fabric.

Milo raised tolerant eyebrows.

'They're supposed to be like that,' he explained. 'For a modern artist you are so out of touch.' He grinned down at her.

'I've better things to worry about than fashion.'

'Everything OK in the world of surrealism? Have you painted any more purple chickens or angels flying backwards?'

Posy delivered a playful punch in his ribs.

'You'll never understand my work, will you?'

'Now, there I agree with you.'

'I'll have you know Montague Wilks has approached me.'

'Seriously?'

'He says my work is a contemporary reflection of modern life.'

'Well done, you! I can't wait to boast about my sister, the world-renowned artist.'

They headed down towards the seafront.

'What news? Did you catch up on old times with your friend, Iris?'

'She didn't turn up.'

'That's a pity. Are you sure you got the day right?'

'I didn't get my dates muddled.'

'Never mind. I expect it'll sort itself out.'

'Milo, I'm worried.'

18

Milo threw a pebble into the sea. Jena raced after it.

'That's old schoolfriends for you, they always let you down.'

'Not Iris. She was head girl.'

Milo pulled a face.

'She doesn't sound my type at all.' He tickled Jena's ears. 'Or yours, come to that.'

'Don't do that.'

'Jena likes being tickled.'

'The sand's wet.'

'Too late.' Milo grinned and Posy watched in despair as Jena rolled over and writhed in ecstasy.

'You're bathing her when we get back,' Posy insisted.

'Anything you say.' Milo nudged Jena with his foot. 'Come on, get up, lazybones. Race you to the breakwater.'

The two of them roared off along the sand, Milo earning admiring glances from two passing females. He was a fit young man and he knew how to use his suntanned looks to best effect.

He eased up and smiled at the girls

lingering by the breakwater, then sauntered over to join them.

Posy watched in envy, wishing she possessed a tenth of his social confidence.

She looked away and shaded her eyes against the sun. Gentle waves lapped the wet sand. This was her favourite time of day when the newly washed sand lay undisturbed.

She picked up a stick and drew a smiley face, feeling her earlier frustration dissolve.

'I've got you a contact at the Palace Hotel,' Milo announced when he returned. 'Ava is a chambermaid and she says if you call on her later today she'll see if she can find out what happened to your friend.'

'Milo, I'm impressed.' Posy stepped back and looked him up and down.

'Younger brothers have their uses. Right, I think I've had enough exercise, so how about lunch? I'll treat you to cod and chips on the pier.'

Later, after Milo had settled down to

watch an afternoon film Posy headed out for the Palace Hotel. Ava was hovering by the entrance to the kitchens.

'Where's Milo?' She looked disappointed.

'He couldn't come,' Posy replied. She hoped his absence wouldn't jeopardise their arrangement.

'Iris Laxton,' she prompted, 'my friend? You said you were going to see if you could find out anything about her.'

Ava drew her reluctant gaze back to Posy.

'Milo's busy, you say?'

'He's on standby.' It was an excuse Posy often used. 'He can't go out in case he's called in to work at short notice.'

Ava sighed.

'He must lead such a glamorous life, flying all over the world.'

'Mmm,' Posy agreed, wondering how she could get Ava back on track. 'Have you discovered anything about my friend?'

'She's checked out.'

Ava turned away from her.

'When?' Posy demanded.

'I don't know but she's not here now.'

Ava looked as though she was rapidly losing interest in Posy and her problem.

Posy grabbed her arm before she disappeared back into the kitchen.

'Do you think I could have a look round?'

'You mean her room?'

'Yes.'

Ava shook her head.

'It's against the rules.'

'Only for a minute.'

'I could lose my job.'

'I'm sure Milo would be very grateful,' Posy coaxed.

Ava hesitated.

'I shouldn't really.' Ava glanced over her shoulder. 'If you absolutely promise you'll only be a minute.'

'No longer.'

'Come on, then.'

Posy followed Ava to the service lift.

She grabbed the laundry trolley and pushed it in front of her.

'In case we're stopped,' Ava explained. 'No-one will look at us twice if we've got the trolley with us. Get in.'

Posy squashed into the cramped space available and Ava squeezed in behind her. The lift clanked its way to the top floor.

'Your friend must have pots of money.' Ava manoeuvred the trolley on to the landing. 'The Roberts Suite.'

She nodded towards the embossed double doors.

'It's got a double aspect, sea view, private sitting-room, king size bed, power shower. We're in luck, the door's open. I'll wait here in case you need me. Don't be long.'

Posy's feet sunk into the deep pile carpet. She could see what Ava meant. Luxury wasn't the word.

She opened the wardrobe. Padded hangers rattled along the empty clothes rail. There was a fluffy hot-water bottle hanging from a hook and two towelling robes.

Not a lot to go on, Posy thought. Time was running out. Ava would be getting anxious.

She peeped into the wastepaper bin. Her interest quickened as she picked out a piece of card. Printed on it in black script was a name. *Stephen Fairfax*.

'Exactly what do you think you are doing?'

Posy spun round and came face to face with Sam Barrington.

# Caught in the Act

The wastepaper bin slipped from Posy's grasp, landed on the carpet and rolled over on to one side. Sam bent down and righted it, giving Posy the chance to slip the card into her pocket.

'I know I shouldn't be here.' She would have tried a smile but the expression on Sam's face wasn't encouraging. 'I was worried. I still haven't heard from Iris.'

'How did you get in?'

It was all Posy could do not to expel a sigh of relief. Ava must have managed to nip back into the lift before Sam spotted her.

'You're right. I shouldn't be here.' Posy avoided the question. 'I'll be on my way.'

She moved towards the door.

'Not so fast.' He stood in her way. 'I want a satisfactory explanation.'

'I haven't done anything wrong.' Posy was equally insistent.

'You're trespassing with intent.'

'Intent to do what?' Posy fired back at him. 'Iris isn't here. She's checked out.'

'How do you know she's checked out?'

Posy bit her lip, annoyed at her silly slip of the tongue. She thought on her feet.

'Isn't it obvious? The suite is empty.'

'I'm going to have to fill out a report. You'd better come down to the office. After you.' Sam held open the door.

Outside, Posy looked up and down the corridor. There was no sign of Ava.

'We'll go the back way.' He indicated the service lift. 'Is this anything to do with you?' He frowned at the laundry trolley.

The lift chose that moment to arrive. A harassed-looking woman emerged.

'There it is.' She grabbed the trolley. 'I've been looking everywhere for fresh towels. We had a temporary chamber-maid on duty this morning and she's left stuff all over the place. Mind if I go down first? I'm way behind schedule.'

Without waiting for an answer she wheeled the trolley into the lift.

'I'll send it back up for you.'

'Does that answer your question?' Posy challenged Sam.

'Not entirely. How did you get up here?'

'I came up in the lift.'

'And just happened to find the door to the Roberts Suite open?'

'That's right. You heard the house-keeper. They had a temporary chambermaid on duty this morning. She must have forgotten to lock the door.'

Sam cast her a sceptical look.

'I've a feeling there's something you're not telling me.'

Posy's fingers curled round the business card in her pocket. Technically she supposed it was hotel property but at the same time it was her only clue to her friend's whereabouts.

'Look.' Posy tried appealing to Sam's better nature. 'Can't we just forget this if I promise not to do it again?'

'Get in,' Sam replied as the lift arrived.

Posy held her breath as they began their descent. To her relief they alighted at the floor above kitchen level. She had no wish to bump into Ava in case the girl gave herself away. Posy didn't want her losing her job over this incident.

Sam's office was small but business-like. On the wall she noticed a professional colour-coded layout of the floor plan of the hotel. The Roberts Suite appeared to run along the entire length of the top floor.

'Is the Roberts Suite your signature room?' she asked.

'It is.'

'So you'd need a lot of money to stay there?'

'More than a security guard earns,' he admitted.

'Do you know if my friend settled her bill before she left or did she just disappear?'

Sam looked surprised by Posy's question.

'I'm only responsible for the security of the premises,' he replied. 'Even if I did know the answer I couldn't tell you. Client details are confidential.'

'All right, then. Here's a question you can answer.' She leaned forward. 'In your experience as an ex-policeman, do missing people often reappear? I mean, do some of them have a mini wobble with life when it all gets too much for them, take some time out and then come back and carry on as if nothing's happened?'

'I take it you're referring to your friend?'

'No-one seems to care that she's missing.'

'But you do?'

'Yes. Iris called me out of the blue and said she had something important she wanted to discuss and was I available to have tea with her?

'I turned up at the appointed time and date but she wasn't here and I can't find out what happened to her.

'She isn't taking calls and I don't know her address because it's been ages since we've seen each other but when I start asking questions I'm being made to feel like a criminal.'

Sam looked thoughtful for a moment.

'How did your friend know how to contact you if you'd lost touch?'

Posy hesitated, then decided to go for it.

'Because I'm famous.'

His reaction was not what Posy was expecting. He threw back his head and laughed with genuine amusement.

'You're not serious?' he managed to ask.

Posy rooted around in her bag for her mobile phone and tapped an app.

'There.' She thrust it under Sam's nose. 'That's me.'

The tips of their fingers touched as

Sam took her phone from her. He scrolled down various examples of her work.

'You paint upside-down trees?' He squinted at the screen.

'Stretches the mind, doesn't it? It's good sometimes to look at things differently. I like to explore the psyche, don't you?'

Sam ignored her question.

'So, you're an artist and that's how Iris got back in touch?'

'The local radio station did a piece on the proposed exhibition of my work and Iris downloaded the podcast.'

'Do people really go in for this sort of thing?' Sam frowned at another of Posy's more vibrant works of art.

'Colour is a marvellous medium. It speaks to everyone and it's great therapy. Art can take on all forms. Don't you feel excited just looking at it?'

For a moment Posy forgot to whom she was speaking until Sam returned her phone.

'I have to admit I thought you protested for a living. I didn't realise you had a proper job.'

'Then this time your policeman's instinct has let you down. I have a social conscience but it doesn't mean I'm not a respectable member of the community.'

'Who isn't above breaking into a hotel suite?'

'I told you — I didn't break in.'

'But you do report friends missing at every opportunity.'

'That's unfair.'

Posy could feel her self-control slipping. Sam Barrington seemed to be going out of his way to disbelieve everything she said.

Unruffled by her reaction he logged into his laptop.

'What are you doing now?' she asked as he tapped various keys before printing out a form.

'You'd better fill this in.'

'What is it?'

'I need a brief account of your

afternoon activities.'

'What happens then?'

'You sign and date it and I log it and put it on file. I suppose I should be grateful to you,' he admitted.

'Why?' She looked up.

'It looks as though I need to review security procedures to make sure the same thing doesn't happen again. People shouldn't be allowed unauthorised access to private rooms.'

Posy signed the form.

'Can I go now?' she asked.

'Yes, but I have to caution you that should the same thing happen again I might not be so lenient.'

Posy stood up.

'And if I want to find out about Iris?'

'Your friend is not my concern.'

'I thought you'd say something like that,' Posy replied. 'What happened to your heart?'

Sam looked taken aback by her question.

'I don't follow you.'

'No, I don't suppose you do. Here.'

She produced a printed flyer.

'What is it?'

'An open invitation to visit Montague Wilks's gallery. Now if you'll excuse me, I need to find out what happened to my friend.'

# Evasive Answers

Posy grimaced. It wasn't easy to concentrate. She didn't want to turn on the overhead lighting but it was growing so gloomy it was virtually impossible to see what she was doing.

Working to a deadline was her least favourite discipline. Art was supposed to come from the soul but these days everything operated as a commercial enterprise and business did not wait for creative muses to strike.

Montague Wilks was a good friend and had offered Posy the chance of a lifetime to display her work to a new and discerning audience but Posy was under no delusions.

Sentiment would not come into the deal. If she failed to deliver, Montague could and would replace her. Seal-bourne was overrun with artists, all prepared to forsake their bohemian

35

principles on the promise of a showing at his prestigious gallery.

Posy knew it wasn't only the gloomy weather disturbing her focus. Any artist of renown could cope with the environment.

It was Iris. Posy couldn't shake off the fear that her old school friend was in trouble.

Iris had been a natural head girl. She was one of those people everyone liked. She was kind, funny, clever and understanding. Two years older than Posy, Iris had taken the younger girl under her wing.

Posy, a rebel, didn't respond well to authority. Teachers preferred rules, not creativity, and Posy frequently fell foul of the system.

Iris had supervised Posy's frequent detention sessions and encouraged her to direct her energy into more positive outlets.

'Don't waste your time doing this.' Iris had pointed to the pages of school rules Posy had been forced to copy out as part of her punishment. 'You need to get out there, take the world by the ears and show it you've arrived and that you're a force to be reckoned with.'

At the time, Posy had resented Iris's lectures. It was only much later after they had gone their separate ways that she realised how Iris had been trying to help her. Now it seemed Iris needed her help.

Posy looked up towards the skylight. Why had she disappeared? Why hadn't she waited to talk to Posy and tell her what was wrong?

A rattle at the front door startled Posy. She hoped it wasn't Montague Wilks. He was a man who stood no nonsense and wasn't above bullying her if Posy continued to ignore his frequent e-mails.

With the chain firmly in place she peered round the door. Sam Barrington hovered on the front step.

'Yes?' she asked in surprise. Sam Barrington was another individual she had no wish to see.

'I need to talk to you,' he said in an urgent voice.

'Has something happened?' Posy opened the door a fraction wider.

Sam turned up the collar of his raincoat to stem the flow of raindrops trickling down the side of his neck. She steeled herself not to weaken and invite him.

'Is this about Iris?' she asked.

'Can I come in? I'm getting soaked.'

His breath misted the air and Posy took pity on him.

'Thank you,' he gasped as she removed the chain from the door.

In the hallway he removed his outer clothing and unlaced his trainers.

'What are you doing?' Posy asked in concern.

'Damp sand sticks to the soles, something it's impossible to avoid in Sealbourne,' he explained. 'And where do you want me to put this?' He looked at his soaking coat.

'It'll dry off in the kitchen. Bring it down here.'

Sam padded behind her into the kitchen where Posy relieved him of his coat and draped it over the airer.

'Thank you. Didn't want to make a mess,' he explained. 'My wife . . . ' He lapsed into silence as if uncertain how to go on.

'You're married?'

'Not any more,' he replied quietly.

Posy knew police work was a major cause of relationship break-ups and she wondered if marital issues were the reason Sam had left the Force.

'Do you drink peppermint tea?' She kept her voice deliberately impassive. Sam's private life was none of her business. 'I usually have a cup this time of day.'

'Thank you.' Sam sat down at the table.

Jena opened one eye and wagged her tail in greeting.

'I need to sign off Iris's file,' Sam explained, 'and I wondered if you had heard anything?'

Posy sat down opposite him.

'Not a word.'

In the comfort of her kitchen Posy felt able to relax more in Sam's company. She noticed a hole in the toe of his sock, and wondered what his houseproud wife would make of that.

'Do you mind if I ask you a personal question?' Sam looked faintly embarrassed as if he too was finding it odd to be relaxed in Posy's company.

'I can always refuse to answer it,' Posy said.

'How did you and Iris lose touch?'

'I don't know, really,' Posy admitted. 'I suppose life got in the way.'

'Do you remember her address?'

'She lived in Littlehurst, a village further down the coast.'

Sam finished his tea and stood up.

'Do you fancy a drive?'

His question wrong footed Posy.

'Where to?'

'Littlehurst.'

'Now?'

'It's my day off and my car's outside.

You're not busy, are you?' Sam asked as an afterthought.

'I'm working on my Montague Wilks commission.'

'Of course.' Sam grabbed up his raincoat. 'Another time, perhaps?'

A sliver of sun broke through the rain clouds and cast a beam across the kitchen.

'Give me five minutes,' Posy said and raced upstairs.

'I like to put the hood down and the rain seems to have passed over. Do you mind?'

Well used to open-air drives with Milo, Posy retrieved an old woollen hat from the pocket of her coat and rammed it on to her head.

Conversation was impossible as they left the seafront and drove inland. The speed of the car whipped up the wind and Posy enjoyed the sensation of fresh air stinging her face and the smell of salt mingled with seaweed.

'Littlehurst.' She tapped Sam's arm and indicated a signpost. Sam nodded and swung the steering wheel to the left.

Posy marvelled at the way he manoeuvred the car round the tight bends, often being forced to back up for farm vehicles coming in the opposite direction and horses being exercised.

Eventually they drew up by Little-hurst village green.

Sam turned off the engine.

'What exactly are we looking for?' Posy asked.

'Clues. Somebody must know Iris.'

'Let's try the church,' Posy suggested.

'The door's locked.' Sam turned the brass handle to no effect.

'Vandalism is a sad reflection of our times,' a voice spoke behind them. 'Locking the door is not something I approve of but we have suffered several thefts. Anthony Johnson,' the man introduced himself, 'vicar of this parish.'

'Posy Palmer,' Posy said.

'And I'm Sam Barrington.'

'Are you on holiday?'

'We're trying to trace an old friend,' Sam informed him. 'We know she used to live in Littlehurst and we'd like to get in touch with her.'

'What was her name?'

'Iris Laxton,' Posy spoke up.

Anthony blinked.

'The Laxtons?' he queried, a wary note in his voice.

'Do you know them?' Posy wondered why the vicar now sounded less friendly.

'The de Villes were one of our oldest families,' he replied.

Posy cast a bemused look in Sam's direction. Had the vicar misheard or was he being deliberately evasive?

'Do the de Villes have a connection to the Laxtons?' she asked.

'Mrs Laxton was the Hon. Serena de Ville before her marriage,' Anthony explained. 'I didn't perform the ceremony, of course. It was well before my time.' He lapsed into silence with a vague smile.

'And Serena was Iris's mother?' Posy persisted.

'That's right.'

'Do any other members of the family live in the village?'

'Gordon Laxton and his wife have regrettably both passed away.'

'Do you know Iris?' Posy's suspicion of the vicar deepened.

'Yes, I know Iris,' he admitted after a short pause.

'Do you know where she is now?' Posy clenched her fists. This was worse than pulling teeth.

'I'm sorry, I don't.'

'What can you remember about the family?' Sam took over the conversation as Posy's line of questioning ground to a halt.

'Mr Laxton was a businessman and travelled extensively.'

Sam waited patiently and after a few moments the vicar continued.

'His wife was in poor health and spent time in Switzerland. I'm sorry,' he apologised, looking at Posy. 'What did you say your name was?'

'It's actually Josie, short for Josephine, but everyone calls me Posy because my brother had difficulty saying Josie when we were little.'

'And you're a friend of Iris?'

'We were at school together.'

'Were you?' There was the faintest spark of interest in Anthony's expression.

'Perhaps you'd like one of my cards,' Posy suggested, 'in case you remember anything else about Iris.'

Anthony glanced at the scarlet tiger stealing through a multi-coloured jungle.

'What unusual artwork.'

'I designed it myself,' Posy replied.

Anthony read the printing on the back.

'I'm not really sure what a surrealist is,' he confessed.

'I suppose you could say we paint alternatives.'

'Now that I do understand.' Anthony broke into his first smile. 'We've showcased some very alternative art-work here at All Saints. I find it helps to connect with younger people.'

Anthony pocketed the card.

'Was there anything else?' He looked at Sam.

'Does the name Stephen Fairfax mean anything to you?' Posy asked on impulse.

Another shuttered expression came over Anthony's face. The church clock struck the hour.

'Is that the time? Sorry, I can't help you any further. I have to go. Please excuse me.'

# Coincidence or Connection?

'You don't think Iris has been kidnapped, do you?'

Sam drew into Fisherman's Courtyard.

'Get real, Posy. Who would the kidnappers ask for the ransom? You heard Anthony. Both her parents are dead.'

'OK, here's another question. Why did Anthony clam up on us?'

'That was odd,' Sam admitted.

'I'm glad we agree on something.'

Sam cast Posy a rueful smile.

'So where do we go from here?' he asked.

Posy, who had opened the passenger door and swung her legs out, swivelled back to face Sam, her nose almost touching his cheek.

'We don't go anywhere,' she replied.

'Yes, we do. I still haven't signed off

47

my file on Iris and I dislike unfinished cases. And who is Stephen Fairfax?'

Posy wished she were better at deceiving people but she knew Sam wouldn't be convinced if she invented a story about him. She'd have to tell the truth.

'I found a card with his name on it.'

'Where?'

'In the wastepaper bin in the Roberts Suite.'

'I wondered why you dropped that bin quicker than a hot cake.'

'So would you have done in the same circumstances. You gave me a fright.'

'I had every right to be there, you didn't — and you do realise that card is the property of the Palace Hotel?'

'I found it and aren't there more important issues at stake than bickering over who has ownership of a card?'

Sam glared at Posy then nodded.

'You're right.'

'Then let's stop behaving like a couple of children and focus on what's important.'

Posy took a deep breath.

'And what is important is to find out why Iris stood me up. Any suggestions? I mean, you must have come across this type of thing more often than me.'

Sam gave it some thought.

'I could see if she had any visitors. They are supposed to sign in but some slip under the radar.'

He cast Posy another look.

'By the way, how did you gain access to the Roberts Suite?'

'That information is on a need-to-know basis.'

'Right, then — if I find out anything about Iris that's on a need-to-know basis too, is it?'

'That's different.'

'Why?'

'She's my friend.'

'And she's my unfinished file.'

'Iris is more than a number on a file. She's a human being and human beings do not disappear for no reason.'

'Some do,' Sam contradicted her, 'but you're right. There's a profile on missing cases and from what you've told me Iris doesn't fit the profile. Unless, of course, there's something else you're not telling me?'

'No,' Posy replied, 'there isn't.'

'In that case I suggest from now on we work together and pool our resources.'

'Deal,' Posy agreed after a moment's thought and slapped her raised palm against Sam's. 'And now I have to get back to work.'

'I'll be in touch,' he replied.

'There you are!' Milo rounded the corner from the direction of his rented lock-up garage. 'I've been waiting ages. I forgot my key. Where have you been?'

'I could ask you the same question,' Posy said, then squealed as Milo enveloped her in a bear hug.

'My flight was cancelled, so here I am. Say you're pleased to see me.'

'Put me down.' Posy battered her fists against his chest. 'I can't breathe.'

Still laughing, Milo released her. In

the background Posy heard a loud roar of an exhaust as Sam accelerated away.

★ ★ ★

'Are you for real?' Milo enquired over plates of lasagne. 'You're going into partnership with Sam Barrington?'

'It's not a partnership,' Posy protested.

'He was the one who arrested you, wasn't he?'

'He didn't arrest me.'

Milo looked unconvinced.

'What were you doing in Littlehurst?'

'It's where Iris used to live.'

'Your old school friend's still gone walkabout, has she?'

'Yes.'

'Did you find out anything in Littlehurst?'

'We bumped into the vicar but he wasn't much help,' Posy replied.

'How about my friend, Ava? Didn't things work out with her?'

'They did — too well.' Posy was

forced into a reluctant admission.

'What do you mean?'

'Nothing.' Posy sighed.

Milo raised an eyebrow.

'You're not normally so edgy. If I were you I should give up looking for Iris. She's causing you nothing but trouble and putting you in a bad mood.'

'That's not the way I see it.'

'You always were a soft touch.'

'Talking of soft touches, Ava was most disappointed when you didn't accompany me to the hotel.'

Milo dismissed Ava's disappointment with a casual wave of his hand.

'It couldn't be helped, but what went wrong?'

'Sam Barrington discovered me rooting through Iris's wastepaper bin.'

Milo's blue eyes twinkled with amusement.

'Did he threaten to clap you in irons?'

'You don't seem to be taking the situation seriously.'

'We didn't get Ava into trouble, did

we?' Milo asked, displaying a late case of conscience.

'Sam knows nothing about her and if you meet him you're not to mention her name.'

'I won't. Flight deck honour.' Milo saluted then glanced at his watch.

'Have you got a date?' Posy asked.

'I do have to be somewhere, like five minutes ago,' he admitted.

Posy wasn't that surprised. Milo was always dropping in unannounced then disappearing just as swiftly.

'Well, it was nice to see you. By the way, you left your shirts up there.' Posy pointed to the airer dangling from the ceiling.

'You've ironed them!'

'They were making the place look untidy.'

'You know, as sisters go, you're not so bad.' Milo beamed and grabbed the pole they used to lower the airer. He paused, his face reddening. 'There's something else I have to tell you.'

'You've got a new girlfriend?'

'I have.'

Posy's brother seemed unusually lost for words.

He took a deep breath.

'Her name is Dulcie Lee.'

'She sounds like a movie star.'

'She works in a library.'

'You're dating a library assistant?' Posy didn't bother to disguise her surprise.

'She's head of Egyptian Artefacts in a redbrick uni. It's a very responsible job. Can I bring her down for a visit?'

'You don't have to ask,' Posy insisted.

'We could go out for dinner.'

'How long have you known Dulcie?'

'I've only just met her, actually,' Milo admitted with an embarrassed smile.

Posy looked hard into her brother's face. She'd seen many of his girlfriends come and go but none of them had warranted a proper introduction and they'd certainly never gone out on a dinner date as a threesome.

'In that case,' Posy said, 'I'm

definitely looking forward to meeting her.'

'You'll love her.'

Milo's face was shining with enthusiasm. He grabbed up his laundry and kissed Posy on the cheek.

A ringtone interrupted them and with his head bent forward to take the call he lowered his voice to a confidential tone.

'Dulcie, hi. How are things?'

With a wave at Posy, he disappeared out of the door, his phone clamped to his ear.

Posy smiled. She hadn't seen this one coming. Milo in love? Unthinkable. He always insisted he enjoyed his bachelor lifestyle too much to settle down.

Shaking her head, Posy wiped her hands. She hoped it wouldn't end in tears.

⋆　⋆　⋆

Up in her studio she made the most of the late afternoon sun. Fired with renewed enthusiasm she worked until the light faded then, with the evening stretching out in front of her and with her mind still on Iris, she went in search of her school yearbooks.

Curled up on the squashy sofa in her small sitting-room, Posy slowly turned the pages until she came to the sixth-form photo. Iris stood tall and confident in the middle of the back row as befitted her status.

Posy got out her magnifying glass. Behind the confident smile her artist's trained eye sensed sadness and she wondered what had been going on in Iris's life at the time.

She studied the girl standing next to Iris, struggling to remember her name. She bit her lip thoughtfully then, extracting the photo from her album, turned it over.

Someone had scrawled names on the back. With a sharp intake of breath, Posy realised the girl standing next to Iris was called Sheila Fairfax.

Was it coincidence or was there a

connection to Stephen Fairfax?

Posy turned the photo over again. She couldn't remember anything about Sheila but she would have been the same age as Iris — two years older than Posy.

Tapping the school details into her laptop Posy was informed that as she didn't have an account she would be denied access to the website. After three abortive attempts to create a strong password the site shut down on her.

Muttering under her breath Posy retrieved the discarded yearbook and flicked through the remaining pages.

She hadn't been allowed to attend the prom concert that year due to her infringement of another of the school rules.

There were several shots of Sheila wearing a gold sequinned ball gown. Iris wore a functional green dress more suited to a garden party, but of the two Posy thought Iris looked more attractive.

One photo showed a laughing Sheila

with her arm linked through Iris's but again the body language was wrong.

Iris's smile lacked warmth. It was as if she wanted to distance herself from contact with Sheila.

Posy picked up the card with Stephen Fairfax's name printed on it and inspected it closely. There was nothing remarkable about it at all.

Why, then, had it been thrown away?

# Mysterious Phone Call

Milo waved at Posy then turned to help his passenger alight. Dulcie was no-one's idea of an Ancient Egyptian scholar. She was petite, with a shiny bob of dark brown hair, beautifully made up and wearing an exquisite dove grey cashmere coat and long black leather boots.

Clutching a soft plum-coloured bag to her chest she looked nervously towards where Posy was standing by the door waiting to greet her.

At that moment the telephone rang.

'Posy?' The voice at the other end sounded uncertain.

Behind her she could hear Milo escorting Dulcie across the cobbled stones.

'Anthony Johnson, vicar of All Saints.'

Posy glanced over her shoulder and

gestured for Milo to take Dulcie through to the breakfast bar.

'Won't be a minute,' she mouthed at them.

'Have I called at an inconvenient time?' Anthony asked.

'I'm expecting guests,' Posy explained. 'How can I help you?'

'I won't keep you long — only I was wondering if you'd had any luck tracking down Iris.'

'None at all, I'm afraid.'

Posy waited for Anthony to continue.

'There's something I omitted to tell you when we met ... two things actually.'

There was another pause before he asked, 'Do you know Iris's real name?'

Posy now knew she was right to be suspicious about Anthony Johnson. If he wasn't on friendly terms with Iris then why was he ringing up to see if Posy had heard from her?

'Laxton,' Posy replied.

'I meant her first name.'

'I always thought Iris was her first name.'

'I found out by accident,' Anthony explained. 'In a parish record,' he added rather lamely, 'I think.'

'What was it?' Posy asked.

'Octavia was Iris's real name. There's no doubt about it,' he said, as if expecting Posy to contradict him.

'Right, well, thank you very much for telling me,' was all Posy could think of to say. 'What was the second thing?' she asked.

'That's a little more delicate and not something that can be discussed over the telephone.'

Posy's interest was now seriously aroused.

'I'm due to attend a symposium but when I'm back could we meet up?' he suggested.

'If you like.'

'Is there anything else I can help you with now?'

'Do you know if Iris has any other living relations we could contact?' Posy wasn't hopeful but as Anthony seemed eager to help she felt it was worth a try.

'She was an only child. She was born to her parents late in life.'

'Surely they don't hold that sort of detail in the parish records, do they?'

'Hurry up,' Milo hissed from the breakfast bar before Anthony could reply, 'Dulcie's dying to meet you.'

'I have to go,' Posy apologised to Anthony.

'What was all that about?' Milo demanded. 'Never mind,' he added. 'Dulcie, this is my sister Josephine, my twin actually, known to one and all as Posy.'

Dulcie blushed.

'Hello.' She extended her hand and Posy shook it.

'I can't place your accent.' Posy frowned.

'Dulcie's originally from the Republic of Ireland,' Milo explained.

'But I've lived in this country for many years,' she added with another shy smile.

'Milo tells me you work in a library.'

'I'm a curator in a university faculty. I spend my days logging artefacts and checking their provenance.'

'Really?'

'You'd be surprised how interesting it is.' Dulcie's face lit up as she talked about her work. 'Every day I discover something new. I love delving into the past.

'You're an artist?' Dulcie ventured to ask when Posy didn't respond.

'I have a studio at the top of the house.'

'That must be interesting, too.'

Milo pulled a face.

'Posy's into surrealism. She's dotty about it.'

'I suppose it's not dotty to have a railway layout in the attic?'

'That's different.'

'Only a man would come out with a comment like that.'

'I'll show it to you, if you like, Dulcie. I've got a proper little village with houses and people and a computer program that regulates the train to whatever schedule I choose.'

'How lovely,' she said with a polite smile.

'Right. Well, I suppose we ought to be going,' Milo said. 'I've booked our table for half past seven. It's at the Palace if that's OK, Posy?

'We've been promised a table by the window. The restaurant has a lovely view across the bay. You'll love it, Dulcie.'

'I'm sure I will,' Dulcie agreed.

'Are you going to change?' Milo eyed up Posy's leggings.

Posy noticed he was wearing a shirt and tie and underneath her coat Dulcie was wearing a pale pink shift that looked the latest line in elegance.

'Perhaps I should,' she agreed.

She mounted the stairs and smiled to herself as she heard Dulcie inviting Milo to tell her more about his railway layout.

★   ★   ★

When they arrived the hotel restaurant was buzzing. A waiter escorted them across the floor to a discreet alcove situated on a raised level by the window. In the background the pianist played gentle mood music.

Milo engineered the seat next to Dulcie and as the waiter held out Posy's seat for her, she saw to her dismay Sam Barrington striding towards them.

'What's the matter?' Milo caught the expression on Posy's face.

'Sam Barrington,' she hissed.

'Hello, there.' Milo greeted Sam with an easy smile. 'I'm Milo Palmer, Posy's younger brother.'

'Only by ten minutes,' Posy put in.

'Of course, you know my bossy big sister,' Milo said, still smiling.

Sam shook Milo's hand.

'I hoped you're being looked after,' he said.

'We've only this minute arrived,' Milo replied, 'but thank you, yes. Everything's fine.'

'I've not seen you in a dress before,'

Sam said to Posy.

'That's in my honour,' Dulcie interrupted with a sweet smile. 'This is my first visit to Sealbourne — Dulcie Lee,' she introduced herself.

'Posy tells me you're head of security?' Milo said.

'Yes, I am.'

'Are you on duty?' Milo asked.

Posy made a face at her brother. She knew exactly where this was going.

'I've just signed off.'

'Then why don't you join us? We can't have poor old Posy playing gooseberry all evening.'

'What a good idea.' Dulcie clapped her hands together.

'I'm sure Sam's tired after his long shift.' Posy did her best to dissuade Sam from joining them.

'And hungry,' Milo added. 'You will join us, won't you? Unless, of course, you have to get home?'

'I live alone,' Sam said, 'in one of the apartments the hotel provides for its staff.'

Before Posy could object further a waiter laid another place at the table. Sam settled down beside her.

'I didn't realise you were a twin,' he said as Milo and Dulcie studied the menu.

'There's a lot about me you don't know.' Posy used her menu to shield her face from her brother and Dulcie.

'Why are you looking so cross?'

'This was supposed to be a family party.'

'Do you want me to leave?'

After a moment's pause and a quick glance across at Milo and Dulcie who were completely engrossed in each other she turned back to Sam.

'No, Milo's right. I don't want to play gooseberry.' She inspected her menu. 'What do you recommend?'

Sam proved entertaining company and throughout the meal the conversation flowed amid much laughter and gossip.

'How did you two meet?' Sam asked Milo.

'Dulcie dropped her bag in the middle of the airport concourse,' Milo explained.

'Corny, I know.' Dulcie giggled. 'But it worked. Then, when we got talking, Milo said he was interested in Ancient Egyptian history.

'Are you all right, Posy?' Dulcie looked concerned as Posy spluttered into her drink.

'Sorry,' she gasped out, 'something went down the wrong way. You were telling me of Milo's interest in Egyptian artefacts?'

She ignored the warning look in Milo's eyes. Anyone more indifferent to Ancient Egypt she had yet to meet, but in the interests of family loyalty she kept quiet.

One of the waiters created a timely interruption by choosing that moment to approach their table.

Dulcie smiled sweetly up at him.

'Ms Palmer?' he enquired.

'That's me.' Posy held up her hand.

He handed over a vivid scarlet scarf.

Posy caught a waft of a delicate fragrance that reminded her of green fields on a summer's afternoon.

'It was left behind by the lady staying in the Roberts Suite. I understand she was a friend of yours?'

Posy cast a glance at Sam.

'May I have a look?' He glanced at the initials embroidered in the corner in silk.

Dulcie, too, leaned forward for a better look.

'OL, those are my initials. My real name is Orla,' she explained. 'Orla means Golden Lady in Irish.'

Milo now took an interest in the scarf.

'Is that so?'

'Dulcie was my father's pet name for me. It means 'love is the sweetest thing'.'

Posy expected an explosive reaction from Milo. He had never been a one for sentiment but his smile never slipped.

Instead he used the scarf as an excuse to touch Dulcie's hand.

'It feels expensive. They have a lot of this type of thing in the Far East.'

'There's some mistake,' Sam now spoke. 'Iris's initials aren't OL.'

'Yes, they are.' Posy fingered the delicate silk. 'Her real first name is Octavia.'

'Octavia — that means the eighth.'

'How do you know Octavia is Iris's real name?' Sam interrupted Dulcie's explanation.

'Anthony told me. He rang tonight,' Posy said, 'just as Milo and Dulcie arrived.'

'Did he tell you anything else?'

'He mentioned that Iris didn't have any brothers or sisters.'

'So she couldn't have been an eighth child,' Milo said. 'How strange.'

'Why did Anthony ring you?' Sam persisted.

'He wanted to know if I'd heard anything from Iris.'

'Who is Iris?' Dulcie asked.

'She's an old school friend of Posy's and she's disappeared,' Milo explained.

'How mysterious. Can I help?' Dulcie enquired.

'What on earth could you do? Sorry,' Posy apologised, 'that sounded rude. I mean, how can you help?'

'I do this sort of thing every day.'

'Tracing lost people?' Sam asked.

'I look into backgrounds. People aren't that much different from ancient artefacts.'

'Looking at Posy I can see a distinct resemblance to an ancient artefact,' Milo teased his sister.

'What I mean is things are often not what they seem.'

'Sounds like a plan.'

To Posy's surprise Sam readily agreed to Dulcie's suggestion as she scribbled down a few of Iris's personal details.

'I'll get back to you as soon as I can.'

'Right, well, the evening seems to be breaking up.' Milo cast a glance around the rapidly emptying dining-room.

'I need to discuss something with Posy,' Sam said. 'I'll see she gets home safely, Milo, if you want to go on ahead.'

Posy wanted to object but Milo seemed more than eager to have some time alone with Dulcie.

'Coffee?' he asked.

'Peppermint tea for me,' Posy said, wondering exactly what Sam wanted to talk to her about.

She was glad of the subdued lighting in the lounge as she sank into one of the comfortable armchairs. Sam reappeared at the same time as the waiter delivered their tray to the coffee table.

'What's that you're carrying?' Posy gestured to the paperwork he held.

'My Iris file.' He sat down and opening it up studied the single sheet of paper. 'I always back up my notes with a hard copy in case the system crashes.'

'You don't have much to go on.' Posy nibbled a miniature macaroon.

'Did Anthony say anything else of importance?' Sam looked up.

'No, but I get the feeling he knows Iris much better than he's letting on.'

'Why do you say that?'

'He knew her real name was Octavia for a start and there's something else he wants to talk to me about when he gets back from his symposium.'

'Have you any idea what?'

'He wouldn't discuss it over the telephone.'

'That is interesting.'

Sam looked thoughtful. He chewed absentmindedly on a square of chocolate fudge.

'Why were you so keen to let Dulcie in on the job?' Posy asked.

'I thought with her experience she might discover something.'

'In an Ancient Egyptian faculty?'

'We haven't done so well tracing your missing friend, have we? She may throw a different slant on things.'

'You agree then that Iris is officially missing?'

Sam drank his coffee and leaned back in his chair, the thoughtful smile Posy was beginning to recognise crossing his face.

'How do you fancy a walk along the cliff tops?' he asked.

# Disturbing Memories

Posy spent an uneasy night as recent events went round and round her head.

'The cliff tops?' she had demanded in reply to Sam's suggestion, determinedly ignoring the chill creep of fear inching up her spine. 'What on earth for?'

Many years earlier she, Milo and their mother had taken a walk along the sea cliff path where they had encountered a severely distressed man standing far too close to the edge.

Her mother had persuaded the man to step back and then spent an hour talking to him as he sobbed out his troubles.

Ever since that day Posy had never enjoyed walking the same path and she certainly had no intention of taking a moonlit stroll anywhere near the cliff edge.

'I'm not suggesting we go now,' Sam

said as if reading her mind.

'Then why are you suggesting we go at all?'

'It's a good place to talk privately.'

'Do we need to talk privately?' Posy asked, distracted.

'Do you have to ask? Iris is your friend and she's disappeared.'

'Why do we have to take a cliff-top walk to talk about her?'

Sam looked uncomfortable and didn't reply.

'Are you saying . . . ?' Posy inspected her empty cup. Her heart beating heavily and her throat aching with anxiety made it impossible for her to finish her question.

She twisted Iris's scarlet scarf through her fingers. Sam touched her restless hands in an attempt to steady them. Posy jumped then stiffened.

'Shall I put your fears into words?'

'Iris hasn't done anything silly,' she insisted. 'She was always so considerate.'

'Who knows what you might do

when you're in trouble?'

'Trouble?' Posy shook her head.

'Perhaps things got a bit much for Iris?'

'If you're thinking of taking a walk along the cliffs to look for evidence that she was up there you won't find any.'

'In all good enquiries you have to cross off every possibility,' Sam spoke in a steady voice.

Posy thought of the poor man her mother had comforted. She dreaded to think what would have happened if they hadn't come along when they did.

'Think about it.' Sam was speaking again. 'Iris said she had a problem that she wanted to discuss with you, didn't she?'

'Yes.'

'And she broke her date. Why?'

'I don't know.'

'And where did she go after she checked out of the hotel?'

'Do you think I haven't asked myself those questions a dozen times?'

The dying flames from the fire

painted ghostly patterns on the carpet. Posy looked down at them, unable to meet the enquiring expression in Sam's hazel eyes.

'It's late,' he said gently, 'and I didn't mean to upset you. Get a good night's sleep. I'll call by tomorrow afternoon if you're not too busy?'

★   ★   ★

Posy clambered out of bed and, shivering in the early morning chill, dragged on her dressing-gown and made her way down to the kitchen.

The sky was streaked with scarlet stripes as the sun began its steady rise. It was a sight that normally lifted her heart but today she had no enthusiasm to enjoy it.

She filled the jug kettle with water and plugged it in. Jena stirred in her basket and obediently trotted into the courtyard through the open back door.

Stifling a yawn, Posy clutched her mug of tea and perching on a bar stool checked her e-mails. There was one from Anthony giving details of his symposium.

There was no mention of the pressing matter he wanted to discuss with her.

Posy poured out a second mug of peppermint tea and, determinedly dismissing Sam's suspicions about Iris from her mind, she picked up her mug and slid off the bar stool.

'I'll be in the studio.' She nodded at Jena who was back snoozing in her basket.

The morning sun pouring through the skylight cast a perfect angle of daylight across the studio and, positioning her easel to maximum effect, Posy commenced work.

Despite her recent troubles her mind was teeming with creativity and she needed to get her ideas down on canvas. She had read somewhere that trouble stimulated the soul and today her paint brush seemed to take on a life of its own as she scored blank canvas after blank canvas with brilliant colours, creating the visionary illusions she loved.

It was nearly lunchtime before noises outside alerted her to the lateness of the hour.

She stepped back, massaging her neck, knowing she had done some of her best work. She would have liked to continue on into the afternoon but she was still in her dressing-gown and needed a shower.

She cleaned her brushes and turned the canvases away from the sunlight streaming in through the main windows.

'Don't be long,' she cautioned Jena, opening the back door into the courtyard. Jena shot outside with a grateful bark.

Showered and changed into a clean smock and leggings, Posy pondered on the reasons why Sam would want a cliff-top conference. Could Iris have done as he suggested and lost her footing and fallen on to the rocks below?

Posy refused to believe that Iris would have fallen on purpose. Besides which, there had been no reports of any recent accidents and wardens regularly patrolled the area.

Something must have happened between the time she telephoned Posy and the time they were supposed to meet up, something that spooked her — but what? Iris was one of the most positive people Posy knew. She wasn't easily rattled.

Jena scuttled back into the kitchen and as Posy closed the door behind her she caught sight of Iris's scarlet scarf draped over a bar stool. Iris loved vibrant colours.

Posy imagined the scarlet would have clashed horribly with her red hair but Iris wouldn't have cared. Her motto had been 'Life Is For Living'.

As if by coincidence the radio was playing a sultry aria. 'Carmen' was Iris's favourite opera. The vivid Spanish background suited her temperament.

When a school trip to see a

performance of 'Carmen' had been proposed Iris had been the first to put her name down.

With her head still in the clouds she had been supervising another of Posy's detention sessions the day after the performance and Posy, looking for an excuse to get out of writing 500 words on the importance of school rules and regulations, encouraged her to talk about it.

' 'Carmen' is a mezzo-soprano role.'

Posy had done her best to look interested.

'What's a mezzo-soprano?'

'Sort of middle range,' Iris explained with an envious sigh. 'I'd love to go to Spain.'

'Why don't you?' Posy asked.

'There are family reasons.' Iris shook her head. 'Aren't you supposed to be doing an essay?' she had added sharply.

Posy put down the scarf and picked up the yearbook that she had left on the kitchen worktop. It fell open at the page showing the photo taken before the choir embarked on the coach for their opera outing.

Ten faces smiled at the camera.

Posy didn't recognise any of them apart from Iris and Sheila Fairfax who again appeared to have positioned herself next to Iris.

Posy dragged her laptop across the breakfast bar. Someone must have kept in touch with Iris. She was one of the most popular girls in the school. It was time to tackle the website again.

With a new acceptable password Posy gained access to the section dedicated to past members of the school choir. She posted a message asking about Iris.

As she logged off she heard a car outside.

Wishing she had never agreed to Sam's suggestion of a cliff top outing but knowing she couldn't get out of it, Posy unhooked Jena's lead off the back of the door and clipping it to her collar the two of them made their way outside.

'Wrap up well, it's windy and the

forecast isn't too brilliant,' Sam advised.

Zipping up her quilted coat and ramming her woollen hat down over her hair and with Jena secure in the gap behind the passenger seat, Posy indicated she was ready. The brisk wind forced her to anchor down her hat with one hand and to hang on to the door handle with the other as Sam took the corners at a brisk pace.

They gained height and scrubby vegetation gave way to chalky outcrops. Sam's car bumped over uneven surfaces before coming to a halt in the designated parking area. He switched off the engine.

The seagulls swooped and dived above them and the wind swished through the scrubby grass.

A volunteer warden wearing a high visibility jacket was seated on a bench outside a hut eating sandwiches. He put down his lunch and strolled over.

'Are you ramblers?' he asked, taking in Posy's inappropriate footwear.

Her shoes were open-toed sandals, not suited to the cliff top terrain.

'I'm asking because there have been one or two incidents lately,' the warden explained. 'Tourists taking selfies. Some of the youngsters dare each other to see how close they can get to the edge. You'd think people would realise the hazards but they never do.

'We have a quiet word in their ear but folk can get quite abusive. Think they know it all, but you look like sensible folk.'

'Are you here every day?' Sam asked.

'A group of us take it in turns. I do the occasional lunchtime stint. Going for a walk, are you?' he asked again.

'That's the idea.'

'Then careful how you go and keep your dog on its lead, madam.' He nodded towards Jena who was now straining at the leash. 'The recent storms have damaged the coast line. Only last week a great chunk fell into the sea.'

'You haven't seen a tall lady with red

hair, have you?' Posy was forced to ask.

'Today?'

'Over the past couple of weeks?'

'I'm not sure. I see lots of people. Up here, was she?'

'Come on.' Sam dragged a protesting Jena away from the warden. 'Thanks for your help,' he called behind him.

'What did you do that for?' Posy was forced to run after him yanking Jena's lead out of Sam's hands.

'We don't want him getting suspicious.'

'What's wrong with that?'

'Nothing — but do you want a repeat of the last time you enquired about a missing person?'

'It may have escaped your notice but Iris isn't an ex-boyfriend and I wasn't enquiring about her.'

'The warden thought you were and we don't want him going official on us.'

'Why not?'

'Because,' Sam explained patiently, 'who's going to believe you when they find out about — what was his name?'

'You mean Barry Grey?'

Posy realised it had been an age since she had even given him a thought.

'He's in the past,' she insisted as a fierce wind buffeted them. 'This is getting us nowhere,' she was forced to shout as the wind increased in strength the closer they got to the edge of the cliff.

She looked round in desperation. There were notices asking people to take care.

In the distance Posy saw the warden approach a group of exuberant youngsters.

The warden grabbed the arm of one young man who had been hopping around on one leg pretending to lose his balance. They laughed at the warden as he tried to make himself heard above the strong wind.

'Let's go and get a hot drink.' Sam's expression was unreadable. 'You're right,' he added. 'There's nothing to see here.'

He tucked Posy's hand through the

crook of his arm. With her other hand clutching Jena's lead, Posy was glad of his support. On shaking legs she allowed him to lead her back down the way they had come.

★ ★ ★

Posy cupped her hands around a comforting mug of hot chocolate. Condensation ran down the windows of the small café nestled in an cove sheltered from the wind. It was a favourite place for dog walkers and hikers sporting maps hung on plastic lanyards around their necks.

Sam ordered two toasted cheese sandwiches and when they arrived at the table he took a hefty bite of his.

Posy followed his example, licking the last crumb of toast off her finger.

'I overlooked breakfast and I missed lunch, too,' she explained.

'You don't like coming up here, do you?'

'No,' Posy said, slightly ashamed that

Sam had noticed her fears.

'Sometimes we have to force ourselves outside our comfort zone. My wife used to say being scared and doing something positive about it helped overcome your demons.' Sam stared at his plate. 'I was in a bad place after I lost her,' he admitted in a small voice Posy hardly recognised, 'three years ago.'

'I'm sorry,' was all Posy could think of to say.

'This Stephen Fairfax?' Sam's brisk response indicated that the subject was closed. 'He isn't Iris's next of kin, by any chance?'

'I have no idea who he is.'

Posy decided not to mention Sheila Fairfax to Sam. The surname might turn out to be nothing more than a coincidence.

'I suppose he wasn't staying at the Palace?' She pushed all thoughts of Sam's wife to the back of her mind.

'There's no record of anyone of that name staying there recently.'

'Do people enter false names? I know they're not supposed to.'

'You'd be surprised what people do.'

'Did you find out if Iris had any visitors apart from me?'

'There were no official ones listed in the visitors' book.'

'We keep coming up against dead ends.' Posy sighed.

'Let's go over what we do know.'

'I've already told you all I know.'

'Then tell me again.'

'Iris called and we made an appointment to meet up.'

'Which she didn't keep.'

'I found a card with the name Stephen Fairfax on it in her wastepaper bin.'

'We also know her real name is Octavia. Have you heard anything from Dulcie?'

'No.'

Sam looked thoughtful.

'If I advised you to drop your investigations, would you do as I suggest?'

'I can't. Iris was good to me when I was going through a difficult phase at school. She never made me feel an outsider.'

'Why should you think you were an outsider?'

'I never fitted in. Everyone else had stable family relationships. My father was an absent-minded classics scholar who often forgot to pick me and Milo up after school.'

'And your mother?'

'She's creative and loves to travel. My father understood that. In their own way they were happily married.'

'Where is your mother now?'

'She lives on a remote Greek island with her partner, Iannis. She wanted Milo and me to go out and live with her after my father died, but Milo was in the middle of his training.'

Posy gave a shaky smile.

'Besides, I don't like olives.'

'What does your mother do on her Greek island?'

'She runs alternative therapy courses

for people who feel the need to get away from the stresses of modern life.

'I know it sounds strange but we love each other as a family even if we don't live together all the time. We need to give each other space.

'The arrangement suits us well. Milo and I share the use of the cottage. He's got a small flat nearer the airport for sleepovers and he comes home whenever he can.'

Posy paused.

'Hardly a conventional background is it? And very different from Iris's. That's why I know she had to be desperate to contact me.'

'Perhaps she knows she can trust you.'

'Then why didn't she keep our appointment?'

There was a biting blast of wind as a group of hikers opened the café door. Posy could hear Jena barking outside.

'We'd better go.' Posy stood up.

'Promise me you'll get in touch if you

hear from Iris.' Sam tugged at the sleeve of Posy's coat.

At that moment Posy felt her mobile vibrate in her pocket signalling an incoming call.

# Enough Is Enough

Back at the cottage Posy settled Jena down in her basket. She hadn't wanted to check her missed call while she was with Sam. There were far too many ongoing issues between them for her to feel happy about fully confiding in him.

Barry Grey featured too significantly in her past for Posy to be sure that Sam believed her fears over Iris.

The missed call was from Dulcie.

'Posy, can you ring me back?' she asked.

Posy ran a hand through her tangled hair. Was this latest event another development it would be wise to keep from Sam?

Hoping Dulcie hadn't discovered more secrets in Iris's past, Posy pressed the recall button. Dulcie answered right away.

'Hi.' Posy did her best to sound upbeat.

'Where are you?' Dulcie asked in a whispery voice.

'Zephyr Cottage,' Posy frowned. 'Why?'

'I don't want anyone to overhear what I have to tell you.'

'Go on,' Posy urged.

'It's about Iris. You won't believe what I've discovered.'

Posy quelled the urge to tell Dulcie not to be infuriating and to get on with it.

'I'm listening,' she coaxed.

'Iris was adopted.'

'Say again,' Posy insisted.

'Her parents weren't her real parents.'

'How do you know?'

'I told you, I'm used to this sort of thing.'

'You had access to Iris's past?'

'Well, let's say I know people who know people and checking the provenance of a vase isn't an awful lot different from checking where someone comes from. Most things are documented. It's a case of looking in the right place.'

'You didn't do anything illegal, did you?'

'Of course not.' Dulcie brushed off Posy's concerns. 'Do you know if she was born in Ireland?' she added.

'I don't know where she was born. Is it important?'

'I was thinking, a lot of adoptions went on in the past — you know, girls giving birth to babies outside of marriage and the families not wanting to keep them because of the shame.'

'Surely all that's changed now?'

'I suppose so.'

'Why do you think Iris might have been born in Ireland?'

'Something someone said during the course of my enquiries.' Dulcie was back to sounding vague again. 'Do you think your friend knew she was adopted?'

'I don't know. Could that fact be

significant?' Posy's interest was piqued.

'Maybe she found out about the adoption and it was a shock, and that's why she wanted to talk to you.'

'There would have been nothing I could do about it,' Posy said, 'apart from provide a sympathetic ear.'

'Perhaps I was right and she was an eighth child.'

'Anything's possible,' Posy acknowledged, wondering where this line of questioning was going.

'None of this really helps, does it?' Dulcie sounded disappointed.

'If you mean are we any closer to finding out what happened to Iris, then no, and whether or not she was adopted doesn't make that much difference to the situation. But thanks for looking into it anyway.'

'Uncovering mysteries is what I do for a living. I found out one other thing.' Dulcie sounded hesitant. 'Strictly unofficial, you understand,' she added hastily.

'Go on.'

'When Iris's father died, the rumour was he left her an inheritance.'

'She's an heiress?'

'I wouldn't go that far.'

'That would explain why she was staying in the Roberts Suite in the Palace Hotel. Ava said it was their best room.'

'Ava?' Dulcie queried.

'She's a chambermaid at the hotel,' Posy glossed over the incident, not wanting Dulcie to discover Milo's involvement.

'You still haven't heard anything from Iris?' Dulcie asked.

Posy decided to play things down.

'I expect she'll turn up and explain it's all been a big misunderstanding.'

'You will let me know if there's anything else I can do, won't you?'

'Thanks, I will.'

'One more thing.'

'Yes?'

'Milo . . . ' Dulcie began.

Posy's heart sank. She could guess what was coming.

'I haven't seen much of him lately.'

'Haven't you?' Posy sounded as casual as she could.

'Is he away?'

Posy tightened her jaw in exasperation. She had been down this route through Milo many times.

She loved her brother dearly but she didn't like covering up for him when it came to ex-girlfriends, and it looked as though Dulcie had fallen into this category.

She frowned, unusually disturbed by Milo's behaviour. Dulcie was a sweet girl. When they'd gone out to dinner at the Palace everything had seemed fine between them.

'Dulcie,' Posy came to a decision, 'I don't want you involved in this Iris thing any more.'

'Why not?' she sounded piqued.

'It's not your affair and I don't feel right about poking into her past.'

'But what about Milo?' she persisted.

'I don't know where he is at the moment,' Posy admitted.

'Can you give him a message from me when you see him?'

'Why don't you call him yourself?'

'He's not taking my calls.'

'Then perhaps you should leave it at that?' Posy did her best to let Dulcie down gently.

'You're trying to tell me nicely that I shouldn't waste my time hanging around waiting for him to return my calls, aren't you?'

'I'm — ' Posy began.

'Thanks.' Dulcie cut her short. 'I get the message.'

Posy felt bad after Dulcie hung up on her and determined to have words with her brother the next time she saw him.

'Come on, Jena.' Posy nudged the dog's soft fur. 'You'd better go out while I prepare supper, then how about an early night?'

\* \* \*

Sam called first thing the next morning. 'Just touching base,' he explained.

Yesterday's storm clouds had blown over and the sun now shone down from a startling blue sky.

Posy had been hoping to have an uninterrupted day at her easel. Her intended early night had turned into a late one as Montague Wilks had called by, demanding to know what progress she had made on her collection.

He'd left her in no doubt of his professional expectations and set her an unbreakable deadline.

Posy knew from experience there was no way Montague would grant her an extension. It was time she knuckled down to do some proper work and not race about the countryside looking for an old friend who probably didn't want to be found.

'Oh, yes?' Posy said now, affecting a casual air. 'About what?'

Sam Barrington was another distraction she could do without.

'Iris,' Sam prompted. 'My file's still open and I don't like unfinished business.'

'Not my problem,' Posy was equally firm in her reply.

'What?' Sam snapped back.

'I've decided to take your advice. If Iris wants to contact me then she knows where I am.'

'What's brought all this on?' he demanded.

'I can't keep running round in circles after someone who doesn't want to be found. I do have a life!'

'What happened to your humanitarian principles?'

'I beg your pardon?'

'Supposing something serious has happened to her?'

Posy clenched her teeth.

'I really don't have time for this, Sam.'

'Is this anything to do with your missed call yesterday? Is that why you're cooling off?'

'I don't know what you're talking about,' Posy hedged.

'I thought we agreed no secrets.'

Posy was having difficulty keeping

her voice under control.

'My missed call was a personal matter and absolutely none of your business. Does that answer your question? Now, if you don't mind, I have work to do.'

Posy turned off her mobile and yanking the lead to the landline out of the wall stomped upstairs.

She probably wouldn't see Sam Barrington again but she needed to remind herself she had taken her eye off the ball with Barry Grey. She mustn't repeat that mistake with Sam Barrington.

Posy spent the day in her studio uninterrupted by calls or visitors. Montague Wilks had every reason to be anxious about her progress. He planned to invest a lot of time and money into her forthcoming exhibition and did not deserve to be let down.

Posy worked on until, too exhausted to raise her paintbrush, she collapsed into her suspended swing chair. Rotating slowly she let her adrenaline return to a normal level.

Visual art could be interpreted in so many ways. People saw things differently and Posy loved opening their minds to alternatives but the creative process could be exhausting.

Her surrealism captured day-to-day life with an explosion of colours and an unusual interpretation that fired the imagination.

A sunset walk with the sky beneath the lovers' feet as they floated along on puffball clouds signified their oblivion to the world around them; a child clutching a jar of psychedelic tiddlers expressed the excitement of a life to come; or a dog racing through long grass pursued by a phalanx of butterflies indicated carefree summer days.

Posy loved her work and Montague's continued sponsorship would ensure that she gained significant recognition.

A rumble from Posy's stomach reminded her she was hungry but she wasn't ready to eat. She could understand why some artists worked for days on end, oblivious to everything else going on around them.

She did a last-minute check of the studio before she opened the door. Jena gave a welcome bark.

'Coming,' she called down the stairs.

The wall clock revealed the time to be half past six. She decided to take in her evening exercise class. Recently Posy had missed several sessions and she now felt the need of an hour's relaxation.

As she registered for the class she noticed someone called Hannah Clarke had e-mailed in response to her request about the school choir.

Too tired to do anything about it for the moment, she headed outside in search of her bicycle.

# Knight in Shining Armour

Posy stared in dismay at her flat tyre. How could that have happened?

She looked round in despair but the car park was deserted. She did not relish the idea of walking home.

Her hair was still damp from the shower and through her thin jacket she could feel goose bumps on her arms. The trees creaking in the wind swayed against the night sky.

The moon peeped out from behind a cloud painting everything a ghostly silver hue. Posy shivered. She had never before realised quite how remote the centre was.

She felt in her jacket pocket for her mobile. It was always possible Milo was around and could drive out and fetch her.

It was then she remembered she had hidden her phone under her comfort cushion, not wanting any interruptions while she had been working.

She straightened her back with a gesture of resolution. There was nothing else for it. She was going to have to walk.

She unchained her bicycle and, dragging it off its stand, began the long trek home. She yelped as the freewheeling pedals banged against her shins. Wrenching the handlebars straight she trundled down the incline towards the park, determinedly ignoring the groups of youths lounging around under the trees.

There had been a lot of trouble recently after dark and a warden regularly patrolled the area. Posy flicked damp hair out of her eyes, limping as her trainers rubbed the bare flesh at the back of her heels.

She paused to catch her breath but laughter and loud music and the sound of drinks cans being kicked around behind her told her the youths were in for a session and it wouldn't be wise to linger.

A beam of light blinded her.

'Who's there?' a voice demanded.

'Posy Palmer,' she stammered.

The warden lowered his torch.

'Sorry, didn't mean to scare you, only it's not a nice night to be out and about.'

'My bicycle's got a puncture,' she explained.

'I can't stop to help,' the warden apologised. 'I need to sort that lot out.'

He nodded towards the disturbance.

'I haven't got far to go,' Posy insisted.

'Take care, then. I'll wish you goodnight.'

Knowing the warden was patrolling the park made Posy's progress easier and a few moments later she emerged into the bright lights of Sealbourne.

'That's a nasty puncture you've got there.' A passer-by inspected her flat tyre. 'It looks like it's been slashed. See here?' The man waggled his finger through the damage. 'If that isn't deliberate I don't know what is. That lot in the park are a menace.'

With her head still spinning and her breath misting the night air that was growing steadily colder, Posy ploughed on. The passageway that led down to Zephyr Cottage from the main street was unlit and she usually avoided it but tonight she had no choice.

The incline made progress easier and she gained speed. The bike juddered over a speed hump, causing Posy to lose hold of the handlebars.

She grabbed out at the saddle but the bike careered off down the hill.

Before she could race off after it she heard the sound of running footsteps. They were gaining on her. She tried to run, too, but her newly formed blister protested and her foot went from under her.

'Don't come near me!' Posy grimaced in pain as her attacker caught up with her. 'I've got one of those spray things.'

'I sincerely hope you haven't, because they're illegal in this country.' Sam

Barrington loomed over her.

'Do you want me to help you up or would you rather I retrieved your bicycle?' he asked.

'What? Why? I don't know.'

'First things first,' Sam extended a hand. 'My mother taught me never to desert a lady in distress.'

'Did she also teach you not to stalk females down dark alleys?'

'I know I should have called out but I didn't want to spook you.'

'Then you failed, didn't you?'

'Where does it hurt?' Sam asked.

'Everywhere.'

Clinging on to his arm, Posy managed to hop into a standing position.

'There's a convenient bit of fence here. Can you lean against it? I won't be a minute.'

'Where are you going?'

'To rescue your bike.'

Posy clung on to one of the palings. Her ankle throbbed relentlessly.

'That looks a pretty nasty puncture.'

Sam wheeled her bicycle back up the incline.

Posy tried to speak but all that came out was a hoarse rasp from the back of her throat.

'Can you walk?' Sam was immediately by her side.

'Just about,' she gasped.

'Hold on to me.'

Together they struggled down the incline and into Fisherman's Courtyard.

'Jena sounds agitated,' Sam said.

Posy eased away from Sam.

'You didn't lock your door,' he said with a frown as Posy pushed it open.

'I don't always remember to take the key,' Posy confessed.

'For goodness' sake, Posy, what planet are you on?'

'Now is not the time for a lecture on security,' Posy snapped back.

'I think it is,' Sam insisted. 'You never know who's hanging around these days.'

'Well the kitchen looks fine to me,'

Posy said as Jena shot out of the door and disappeared around a darkened corner.

'Go after her.' Posy flapped her hands at Sam.

'I can't leave you.'

'Yes, you can.' Posy clung on to the wall then hopped over the threshold grabbing on to work surfaces before lowering herself on to a kitchen chair.

Sam returned moments later clutching a wriggling Jena.

'Want me to wipe her paws?' he asked.

Posy watched Jena sniffing Sam's jumper as he tended to her with a towel.

'Right, now let's see to you,' Sam said as he finished the task in hand.

'My paws are fine, thanks,' Posy retorted.

'Jena, basket,' Sam instructed.

Jena pattered obediently across the floor and nestled down on her blanket.

Sam kneeled in front of Posy and took her ankle in his hand.

'This is going to hurt but I need to

take off your trainer. I'll be as gentle as I can.'

Posy stared determinedly at the wall as Sam ripped the Velcro open then eased her trainer off her swollen foot.

'OK, you can relax.'

'What are you doing now?' Posy demanded.

'Inspecting your injury. I don't think anything's broken but it's going to be tender for a day or two and you'll need to put something on that swelling. Here.' He pulled another chair over. 'Rest your leg on that.'

Posy heaved her leg on to the cushion.

'Thank you,' she mumbled.

'You need some hot sweet tea.'

Too tired to raise further objection, Posy watched Sam sort out cups and plates.

'Have you eaten anything?'

'Not for a while.'

'Sandwich?' He held up a chunk of cheese.

Posy realised in spite of her injury she

was very hungry. It was hours past her usual suppertime.

'The salad bits are in the bottom of the fridge.' She pointed in the direction of the fridge freezer.

Sam began poking around.

'What have we here?' He nudged a plate of millionaire's shortbread towards Posy. 'Never could resist these,' he said, helping himself.

In the warmth of the kitchen Posy's limbs thawed out. She flexed her tingling fingers and wriggled out of her rain soaked jacket.

'Here, let me.'

Sam leaped forward to help. He draped it over the range.

'Do you need a towel?' He grabbed one off the airer and handed it over.

Posy patted her damp hair.

'Why were you following me?' she asked.

'I wasn't.'

'Do you usually lurk around dark alleys in the rain?'

'The park warden is a retired police

officer. He said that there might be some trouble later tonight so I decided to offer him moral support. He mentioned bumping into you and that you looked as though you could do with a helping hand.'

'And like a white knight you came rushing to my rescue?' Posy found it impossible to keep the sarcasm out of her voice. 'Sorry,' she added, 'that was mean of me. I am grateful.'

'I made things worse, didn't I?' Sam shook his head, avoiding her eye, and began searching for bread.

'You've cut yourself!' Posy noticed a trickle of blood on his forehead.

'What?' He looked startled.

'Your head, it's bleeding.'

Sam ripped a sheet of paper towel off the roller.

'There was a scuffle in the park with some of the youths.' He dabbed at the wound. 'Things got a bit lively.'

'But you're all right?' Posy was surprised at how concerned she felt.

'It died down when the community

115

officer arrived. That's when I came looking for you.' Sam threw the used paper towel into the bin.

'You'll need to put a dressing on it,' Posy insisted. 'Right-hand cupboard above you.'

A rumble of thunder in the distance was accompanied by a low growl from Jena.

'There, there,' Posy soothed.

Jena wagged her tail and settled back in her basket while Sam fumbled with a plaster.

'I never could get the hang of these things.' He looked up in frustration as more blood trickled from his head wound.

'Bring the first-aid box over here.'

'I can manage,' was Sam's stubborn reply.

'No, you can't — and stop sounding like me.'

'Heaven forbid.'

'You're not a very good patient, are you? Sit still,' Posy insisted as she wiped Sam's forehead and applied the plaster.

'There, now we've dealt with each other's injuries, where's the tea?'

Sam loaded up the tray and carried it over to the coffee table.

'What's so amusing?' he asked.

'We are. Anyone looking through the window would wonder what on earth we had been up to, you with your bandaged head and me with my swollen foot.'

The corner of Sam's mouth curved into a smile. Posy wished the bandage didn't make him look quite so rakish.

'Tuck in,' he urged. 'I wonder how your tyre came to be punctured,' he added through a mouthful of cheese,

'Do you think it was deliberate?' Posy's eyes watered. Sam had used the strongest cheese, the one she usually kept for her three-cheese pasta.

'I spoke to a man outside one of the restaurants,' she explained when she'd finished coughing. 'He seemed to think it had been slashed on purpose and that the youths in the park might have done it.'

'It's possible — unless you can think of someone who has a grudge against you.'

'It can't be anything to do with Iris, can it?' Posy asked in an uncertain voice.

'I thought you'd given her up as a lost cause.'

Posy's eyelids drooped as the drama of the evening caught up with her.

'We'll talk about it another time.' Sam cleared away the plates. 'Can you manage the stairs?'

Posy finished her tea, then stifled a yawn behind the back of her hand.

'The sofa pulls out into a bed. I'll sleep downstairs tonight, then I'll see how I feel in the morning. Can you let yourself out?'

Sam hesitated as if he were about to raise an objection, then nodded.

'Make sure you lock the door behind me.'

'I will,' Posy reassured him.

Later, as Posy drifted off to sleep, she realised Iris's scarlet scarf was missing from where she'd draped it over a bar stool.

# Shock Discovery

In the morning Posy's ankle was swollen and discoloured but as long as she didn't put too much pressure on it she was able to hobble around.

Seated at the breakfast bar she went through her e-mails. She still hadn't answered the one from Hannah Clarke.

Briefly thanking Hannah for her response she added her mobile telephone number and pressed *send*. A quick scan of her inbox revealed there had been no other responses to her request for contact from choir members who remembered Iris Laxton.

Briefly updating Montague Wilks on her mishap, she quickly reassured him her folio would be ready on time. Montague had sounded waspish, leaving Posy with the uncomfortable feeling that he didn't really like artists but had to put up with them for the sake of his business.

Her mobile signalled an incoming call from a number she didn't recognise.

'Posy Palmer? Hi, Hannah Clarke here.'

'Hannah. Yes. Hello. Thank you for calling.' Posy stumbled over her response.

'I didn't expect you to get back to me so soon.'

There was a short pause as if both of them were assessing the situation.

'Did you get much response to your request for news about Iris?' Hannah asked.

'So far you've been the only one.'

'Iris didn't really keep in touch with anyone special,' Hannah said.

'But you did?'

'I wasn't in the choir but we were close for a time. I couldn't sing to save my socks — unlike Iris.' Hannah laughed. 'You were a year or so behind us, weren't you? Do you remember me?'

'I'm sorry, I don't.'

'I did rather blend into the background but I remember you.' Hannah still sounded amused. 'You were always in trouble because your skirt was shorter than regulation length and you hated wearing the uniform white blouse.'

'I still hate white blouses.'

'And it was you who was responsible for drawing Miss Bircher looking like a hedgehog, wasn't it?'

Posy flushed. It had been a cruel trick to play on the art teacher, even if she had been scathing about Posy's alternative interpretation of a rural idyll.

Posy had chosen to portray the countryside in a less than romantic way. Her drawing showed how man's thoughtlessness could destroy nature.

It had been a powerful piece of work of which Posy had been proud, but Miss Bircher had not appreciated its message. She had held Posy's work up in front of the whole class and roundly criticised it.

In retaliation Posy had done a sketch

of Miss Bircher camouflaged as a hedgehog with rainbow-hued fluorescent prickles and a glowing pink snout. She'd entitled it 'Radio Active' and pinned it in the centre of the entrance-hall notice board where it had attracted maximum exposure.

'It was brilliant,' Hannah enthused. 'So why are you trying to get in touch with Iris?'

'It's a long story,' Posy admitted.

'Look, can I come round now? I'm in Sealbourne. You live in Fisherman's Courtyard, don't you?'

Posy still had no recollection of a Hannah Clarke and some of Sam's security lecture had rubbed off on her. She was convinced the disappearance of Iris's scarf was no accident and she was equally convinced that someone had been in the cottage while she had been at her exercise class.

'How do you know my address?' Posy asked in a guarded voice.

Hannah's laugh was beginning to grate on her nerves.

'I downloaded your app.'

'It doesn't give out my private address.'

'Doesn't it? I have to say your work is amazing. I'm always boasting to my friends that I was at school with you. I'll be with you in a quarter of an hour.'

Posy finished the call, wondering if she should update Sam on this latest development. She decided against it. It would probably turn out that all Hannah wanted was a girly chat about their schooldays.

Carefully manoeuvring her way across the kitchen she unlocked the back door and inhaled the tang of seaweed carried inshore by a sharp wind blowing off the sea. Winter was on its way. Posy shivered and turned back inside to grab a jumper.

A car drove into the courtyard and she watched a tall blonde woman emerge.

If this was Hannah Clarke she was hardly dressed for a day at the seaside. Her low cut sparkly top and fitted tight black trousers, paired with designer sandals, were more suited to a fashionable cocktail party.

'Hi there, Posy.' She teetered over the cobblestones on her incredibly high heels. 'You look fantastic.'

She air-kissed Posy's cheek.

'Have I got a smut on my nose?' she asked when Posy didn't move.

'I, um, yes, I mean no, come in.' Recovering herself, Posy limped away from the door to allow Hannah to pass.

'What have you done to your ankle?' Hannah sympathised. 'Fallen over a bucket and spade?' Her ruby red lips parted in a smile to reveal perfect white teeth. 'And who's this?'

She bent down to pat Jena who had come to the door to see what all the excitement was about.

'Aren't you the business?'

Jena tickled Hannah's bare toes with her cold nose then pattered back to the warmth of the Aga.

'Was that contraption anything to do with your injury?' Hannah indicated

Posy's bicycle that Sam had left propped up against the wall.

'Sort of,' Posy replied.

'I was hearing about the trouble in town last night. You weren't part of it, were you?' Not waiting for an answer, Hannah's brown eyes reminded Posy of a robin's as they darted around the kitchen.

'Still up to your activist tricks, I see.' She pointed to one Posy's old banners draped above the Aga. 'Sit down,' she urged as if she were the hostess, 'and tell me where everything is. I'll get coffee on the go.'

'Peppermint tea for me,' Posy insisted.

'Anything you say.'

Hannah put her handbag on the bar. 'Cosy place you have here.'

'How did you find out where I live?'

'Iris told me,' Hannah replied.

'You've seen Iris?' Posy demanded.

'I'll be with you in a few minutes. Milk? Here we are,' she said, not waiting for Posy's reply. 'You know,' she smiled, 'you haven't changed a bit.'

She kept up a constant stream of chatter as she boiled water and sorted out mugs.

'You're how old, now?'

'Twenty-five,' Posy answered.

'I usually admit to twenty-two but I can't very well do that with you, can I?'

She brought the drinks to the table and settled down opposite Posy.

'I suppose I'd better start from the beginning — unless you want to go first? Hey, isn't that the school year-book?' She grabbed it off the dresser. 'I don't know what happened to mine.'

Hannah flipped open the pages and smiled as the recognised old faces.

'There's Iris, and that's me next to her.'

Hannah pointed to the girl wearing a gold ball gown. Posy leaned forward.

'Surely that's Sheila Fairfax, isn't it?'

'That name brings back memories.'

⋆   ⋆   ⋆

Hannah grimaced. 'Everyone was called Sheila way back then. With six Sheilas in our class I decided Hannah, my second name, sounded much more sophisticated, so as soon as I could I changed it.'

'And Clarke?'

'I was married.' Hannah's tone indicated it was not a subject she wanted to discuss.

'Are you, by any chance, related to Stephen Fairfax?' Posy hardly dared ask the question.

Hannah eyed up the shortbread.

'One finger can't do much harm, can it?' She nibbled daintily around the edge of the caramel topping.

'Stephen Fairfax?' Posy persisted.

'He was my brother.'

'Was?' Posy's heartbeat quickened.

Hannah put down her piece of shortbread.

'He died.'

'I'm sorry.'

Hannah gave a shaky smile.

'Thanks.' She lapsed into silence and

sipped her coffee.

'I'm trying to contact people who knew Iris,' Posy explained, seizing her chance.

'Right,' Hannah said. 'May I ask why?'

She's disappeared.'

'What?' Hannah slopped coffee into her saucer.

'We had a date to meet up. She didn't keep it and I can't find out what's happened to her.'

'She was staying at the Palace Hotel.'

'She's not there now.'

'She must have moved on.'

'Then why hasn't she been in touch?'

'Good question.'

'Also, there was a card in the wastepaper bin in her room.'

'Oh, yes?'

'It had your brother's name on it.'

'Stephen's?'

'Yes.'

'This is getting seriously weird.'

'You don't know anything about it?'

'Why should I?'

'You're in the area. Stephen is your brother and you knew Iris was staying at the Palace Hotel.'

'Hold on a minute,' Hannah spoke slowly and carefully, 'aren't you getting a little ahead of yourself?'

Posy's ankle throbbed as if warning her to slow up.

'Did your brother know Iris?'

An uneasy look crossed Hannah's face.

'Yes, he did.' She held up a hand. 'You've had your say, now it's my turn.' She ran a hand through her casually disarranged hair, then took a deep breath. 'Did you know Iris's mother suffered from poor health?'

'Yes,' Posy replied.

'Iris's father took her abroad to Switzerland but unfortunately there was nothing that could be done for her. I sent Iris a message of sympathy. Are you with me so far?'

'Go on,' Posy urged.

'I suppose Iris was feeling lonely or something. Anyway, she replied, inviting me to spend a few days with her at her place down in the country. Hammer Pond House, it was called. Do you know it? It's huge. No wonder she wanted company.

'I hadn't passed my test at that time, so Stephen volunteered to drive me down. He was on leave from the army and at a bit of a loose end. He and Iris clicked and Iris invited us both to stay over. Everyone got on like a house on fire and I could see Iris was perking up in our company.

'In the end we stayed for over two weeks. We had a great time.'

'And that was the last time you saw Iris?'

'No, we had tea together in her suite in the Palace Hotel.'

'You had tea with Iris? Was she worried about anything?' Posy asked.

'Not that I noticed. We chatted about old times. It was a pleasant afternoon.'

'Do you live in Sealbourne?' Posy asked.

Hannah looked amused by the idea.

'I'm a city girl. Give me bright lights and a pavement under my feet every time.'

'Are you on holiday?'

'Wrong again. I'm here with my boss. I meet and greet people on his behalf and do all the things involved with arranging conferences. He's researching the area for new places to host corporate events.

'That's how I bumped into Iris — literally. She was walking along the promenade taking the afternoon air.'

'And that's it?' Posy asked.

'There's not much more I can tell you. When I left Iris she was fit and well.'

'Did she mention me?'

'Only in passing.'

'And you really have no idea why she would possess a card with your brother's name on it?'

'I might have.'

Posy's suspicions were aroused by Hannah's embarrassed smile.

'How well did Iris know your brother?'

'I suppose you could say better than some.' Hannah paused before blurting out, 'She married him.'

# Unexpected Development

Posy had to talk to Sam Barrington and what she had to say couldn't wait.

The cab drew up outside the Palace Hotel.

Gaia was on duty and greeted Posy with a friendly smile.

'I'll inform Mr Barrington you're here.'

Sam strode into the lounge a few minutes later, subjecting Posy to such intense scrutiny her cheeks reddened.

'How's your ankle?'

'I haven't come here to talk about my ankle.' Her impatience resurfaced. 'There's been a development.'

'I hope you remembered to lock up before you left?'

'Of course I locked up and I've left Jena guarding the premises. Are you listening to me?' She knew her face was flushed.

'You need to calm down,' Sam insisted.

'I'm perfectly calm.'

'Then what's made you rush over here?'

'I had a cup of tea with Hannah Clarke.'

Sam settled into one of the wing-backed chairs.

'I think you'd better start from the beginning.'

Sam listened attentively, not interrupting until Posy finished her account of the morning's events.

'And your problem is?' he asked slowly.

'Something isn't right.'

'With this Hannah?'

'With everything. Iris's scarf is missing, too.'

'Her scarlet scarf?'

'I left it draped over a bar stool and it's not there any more.'

'Jena hasn't hidden it somewhere?'

'She hasn't done anything like that since she was a puppy.'

'Maybe she's a fashionista dog.'

'If you're not going to take me seriously,' Posy said, wriggling in her seat trying not to put any weight on her ankle, 'I can do this on my own.'

'Sit still,' Sam insisted. 'You're not doing anything on your own. I'm on your side, remember?'

'Sometimes I wonder.'

'Why has Hannah put you on edge?' Sam asked patiently.

'She's glib, glamorous and she was clinging on to Iris in the school photo.'

'Serious.'

'And she's changed her name.'

'Iris has got two first names, you don't use yours,' Sam pointed out, 'and don't forget Dulcie. You'll have to give me more than that.'

'What about Iris's scarf?'

'When did you first notice it was missing?'

'Last night.'

'And you've no idea who could have taken it?'

'Milo's away. Montague Wilks is

always popping in but he would have no reason to take a scarf. What about Hannah?'

'I thought you said she visited this morning?'

'She knows where I live. She could have dropped by last night while I was pushing my bicycle home.' Posy's blue eyes rounded in speculation. 'You don't think she punctured my tyre, do you?'

'Get a grip, Posy.'

'Have you a better suggestion?'

'Not right now,' Sam admitted. 'Apart from punctured tyres and missing scarves what other leads have we got?'

'Anthony Johnson.'

The heat from the coal fire continued to warm Posy's face, that and the searching look Sam was giving her.

'If he's back from his symposium let's invite him over here. Once he's relaxed in front of a good fire I think he might be more forthcoming and tell us what he knows. May I?'

He picked up Posy's mobile and

scrolled down the contacts.

'Here we are.'

He quickly tapped in a message and a reply to his text pinged back within moments.

'He's on his way.'

'Do you think we're getting somewhere?'

'It's a step forward. Now before Anthony arrives have you anything else to report? You can start with Hannah Clarke. What do you know about her?'

'It's definitely her in the school photo although in those days she was going by the name Sheila Fairfax.'

'And she was Iris's sister-in-law?'

'So she says.'

'We can check that out. And her brother? The one who was married to Iris, what do we know about him?'

Posy shook her head.

'I know he was in the army, and he has to be older than Hannah because he'd passed his driving test and she hadn't.'

Sam glanced over Posy's right shoulder towards the reception desk and frowned.

'That's strange,' he said.

'What is?'

'I could have sworn your friend, Dulcie, has just walked through reception.'

Posy swivelled round.

'Would she be visiting Milo?'

'Dulcie hasn't seen much of Milo lately,' Posy admitted.

'You've heard from her?'

'She telephoned with the results of her investigations into Iris's background.'

'Something else you forgot to mention?' Sam enquired.

Posy didn't think it was possible for her face to get any redder.

'What she told me was personal to Iris.'

'Personal or not, if you want me to help you I need to know what's going on.'

'Dulcie found out that Iris was adopted,' Posy admitted, 'but I fail to see how that can have anything to do with her disappearance.'

'Let me be the judge of that.'

'There's no need to adopt interview-room techniques.'

'Did Dulcie discover anything else?' Sam asked in a patient voice.

'She seemed to think there might be an Irish connection and it is possible Iris's father left her a substantial inheritance.'

'Now that is interesting.'

'Why?'

'Follow the money.'

'Somebody could be after her inheritance?'

'It's a possibility.'

'If Dulcie's right about Iris's adoption maybe her real family are trying to trace her.'

'You're thinking like a detective,' Sam encouraged. 'Go on.'

'If they've found out she was an heiress we have a motive.'

'For what?'

'Hello, there.'

Posy jumped at the sound of a voice behind her. The doorway to the lounge was so low Anthony had to duck to avoid hitting his head on the beam.

'Can I come in?'

He was dressed in jeans and a chunky sweater over his dog collar. He pushed his glasses up the bridge of his nose and gave a nervous smile.

Sam leaped to his feet.

'Anthony.' He shook him by the hand. 'Good to see you again. Take a seat.'

'I came over as soon as I got your message,' Anthony explained as he shrugged off his backpack and settled down.

One of the waiters hovered.

'Nothing for me,' Anthony insisted, 'I can't stay long, sorry.'

He gave another nervous smile.

'I've such a backlog of stuff to get through. You wouldn't believe how things mount up when you're away even for a few days.'

'In that case let's get down to it.

What have you got for us?' Sam said.

'I should have told you before, only I was in a quandary. This sort of thing is seriously outside my experience. I can rely on your discretion?' He spoke in a rush.

'It goes without saying,' Sam replied.

'Have either of you heard from Iris?' Anthony looked at them hopefully.

''Fraid not.' Posy shook her head.

'Neither have I,' Anthony admitted.

Posy frowned.

'I didn't realise you were that close.'

Anthony fiddled with the sleeve of his jumper, pulling at a loose woollen thread.

'What I failed to tell you is that about six months ago Iris came down to Littlehurst to All Saints. She was the soloist taking part in a lunchtime recital given by a chamber choir. Did you know she is a talented mezzo-soprano?'

'I knew of her interest in music. She used to tell me all about opera and the roles she would like to perform,' Posy replied.

'The visit was a great success and we had a small reception afterwards and the choir agreed to give further recitals.

After everyone had drifted off, Iris and I began talking and we arranged to go out for a meal. Iris occasionally caters for private dinner parties and she likes to check out other establishments. It means she can work as and when she likes.

'Anyway, she'd heard of a local restaurant that was receiving rave reviews so we went there for dinner. Over our meal we relived old times, how much Littlehurst had changed, that sort of thing. We got on so well that we arranged another date in another restaurant, and one thing led to another.'

'Are you telling us you're in a relationship with Iris?' Sam asked.

'Of a sort.' The shuttered look came over Anthony's face again.

'Why didn't you say so earlier?' Posy wanted to know.

'I don't know. I have to admit I was

cross with Iris for taking off without a word — not a very adult emotion, I know.'

'Why did she take off?'

'We had a falling out. It was so unlike Iris. We never quarrel but it was almost as if she engineered it. I can't even remember what it was about now.

'She said she wouldn't be in touch with me for a while because she had something she needed to sort out. When I pressed her she wouldn't be drawn as to details but insisted I wasn't to contact her and that I wasn't to worry. But of course I'm worried about her. She means everything to me. If something was bothering her why didn't she want to tell me about it?'

'Why indeed,' Sam agreed.

'Did you know Iris was adopted?' Posy asked.

Anthony hesitated.

'It's not something she talked about.'

'But you did know?'

'Yes, I knew.'

'Did you also know about her

marriage to Stephen Fairfax?' Sam asked.

Anthony heaved another sigh.

'Only recently. Again, it was not something Iris liked to talk about.'

'There seem to have been quite a few secrets in Iris's life,' Sam said.

'Iris is a lovely girl.' Anthony leaped to her defence.

'No-one's saying she isn't,' Posy soothed him. 'We're only trying to get to the bottom of what's going on.'

'Do you know how Stephen Fairfax died?' Sam asked.

'In an accident.'

'And where does Iris live now?' Posy decided to pursue a different line of questioning.

'She's in the process of selling her flat,' Anthony said. 'Then she'll move into the vicarage?'

He looked embarrassed then relieved when Sam interrupted.

'There's something you can do for us.'

'Anything.'

'Could you ask around Littlehurst to see if anyone's seen Iris?'

'I told our community police officer in confidence about Iris. She said many people who disappear often don't want to be found, but that isn't like Iris, is it?' Anthony appealed to Posy.

'Well, there's not much more we can do for the moment.' Sam filled the awkward silence that followed.

'I think there is,' Anthony said, sounding surprisingly firm.

Sam raised his eyebrows.

'What?'

Anthony leaned down and retrieved his backpack off the floor.

'This was thrust through the vicarage letter-box some time within the last twenty-four hours.'

He rummaged in his bag and produced a crumpled package. He shook it open.

Posy stared in disbelief as Iris's scarlet scarf tumbled across the table.

# A Comforting Kiss

Posy buried her face in the scarf and inhaled its delicate French fragrance. She didn't want Sam to see her distress.

'You are sure this is Iris's scarf?' Sam looked hard at Anthony.

'I had it especially commissioned for her birthday. See, it's got her initials in the corner — OL.'

'Octavia Laxton,' Sam confirmed. 'Even though everyone calls her Iris?'

'She sings under the name Octavia Laxton. She said she thought it sounded more in keeping with the status of a mezzo-soprano. I used to tease her about it.'

'So you didn't find her name in a parish record. Are you usually so economical with the truth?' Posy demanded.

'Sorry. I'm all over the place at the moment.' Anthony blew his nose, causing Posy to immediately regret her outburst.

'I understand. I was fond of her, too.'

'Was?' Anthony picked up on the past tense and lowered his voice to a whisper. 'You don't think the worst?'

'You didn't see who put the scarf through your door?' Sam interrupted before Anthony became too distracted.

Anthony shook his head.

'It could have been anyone. On an average day I get anything up to fifty visitors. I operate an open-house policy.'

'There was no message with it?'

'Nothing.'

'Does the scarf have any other special significance?'

'Iris used to like to swirl it around her neck before she made an entrance for one of her performances, but that's not much to go on, is it?'

'And you haven't heard anything else from anybody?' Sam asked.

'Not a word. There has to be an innocent explanation to all this, doesn't there?'

Posy decided not to tell Anthony that the last time she had seen Iris's scarf, it had been draped over a stool beside her breakfast bar.

'If only we hadn't fallen out!' Anthony sounded distressed.

'It's not your fault.' Posy did her best to comfort him.

'I'd best be going.' Anthony picked up his backpack and slung it over his shoulder. 'Please,' he appealed to Sam, 'find her for me.'

'I've got to go, too,' Posy said.

'I'll drive you back,' Sam offered.

Neither of them spoke during the journey. Posy didn't know what to say and Sam appeared lost in his own thoughts.

As they approached Fisherman's Courtyard Sam swerved to avoid a car slewed across the entrance.

'Milo's home,' Posy said.

'I hope he's better at flying aircraft than parking a car.' Sam negotiated the limited space available. 'Do you want me to help you inside?' he asked.

'I can manage,' Posy insisted.

'What are you going to do about this?' Sam lifted a corner of the scarf Posy was still clutching.

'I need to think things through.'

'Don't leave it too long.'

'I can't help feeling sorry for Anthony. He looked so lost. I hope Iris hasn't walked out on him.'

'Or worse.' Sam echoed Anthony's fears.

'You don't think the cliffs have anything to do with her disappearance, do you?'

'Right now I feel like Anthony — all over the place,' Sam admitted.

Unable to look at him in case her composure collapsed, Posy turned away.

Sam did think something had happened to Iris, something serious.

Taking a breath to steady her nerves, Posy opened the passenger door. As she did so she felt a sensation at the base of her neck.

She swung back to face Sam. He

jolted away from her.

'What are you doing?'

'Kissing you,' he admitted with a self-conscious smile.

'Why?'

'After all the drama of the morning I thought we both needed some creature comfort, but from the look on your face I'm not so sure it was a smart move.'

Posy hesitated for a fraction of a second, unsure how to respond.

'You could have chosen a better moment,' she said.

'Does that sort of thing go against your feminist views?' Sam enquired.

'Feminism is an unnecessary word in a modern world,' Posy insisted.

'If you say so. Anyway I thought you'd given all that up now you're a successful artist.'

'I'll never give up fighting for the rights of the individual, male or female.'

'I'm pleased to hear it.'

'For the moment Iris is my cause,' Posy insisted.

'Then let's keep it that way — for the

moment,' he added.

'I must go.'

Posy swung her feet out on to the pavement.

'Mind your ankle,' Sam called after her as Posy struggled out of the car and clung on to the door to steady her shaky legs.

★ ★ ★

A strong smell of toast greeted Posy as she opened the kitchen door.

Milo was standing by the grill.

'Did I see Sam Barrington?'

'Yes. He gave me a lift.'

'Again? He seems to be making a habit of it. Want some?' He pointed to his snack.

'Hey,' he said, noticing his sister's limp, 'what did you do? Not another protest?'

'It's a long story but I need you to mend a punctured bicycle tyre.'

'I won't ask how or why,' Milo said. 'Sit down and I'll serve up and you can

152

tell me what's been happening in my absence.'

'I had a call from Dulcie. Milo,' she demanded, 'what's going on?'

'Nothing,' he mumbled through a mouthful of toast.

'She said you're not taking her calls.'

'You know me — fancy free.'

'There's more to it than that, isn't there?'

Milo refused to look her in the eye.

'Out with it.' Posy used the tone of voice that always made Milo crumple.

'I don't like being two-timed.' He sounded like a disappointed small boy.

Posy's fork slipped from her fingers.

'Dulcie's two-timing you?' she repeated in shocked surprise. 'Good for her.'

'That's not very sisterly.' Milo looked affronted. 'I thought you'd be on my side.'

'I am, little brother.' Posy patted his hand, still smiling at the irony of the situation. 'How do you know that Dulcie's got another man?' she asked, intrigued.

'I saw them together.'

'What was he like?'

'From the back he looked about thirty, stocky, dark-haired. I couldn't see his face — it was turned away from me.'

'Where was this?'

'A coffee bar near the faculty. I was paying a surprise visit. She didn't see me.'

'And?' Posy prompted.

'The man was giving her a big hug, that's why I couldn't see his face.'

'He could have been anybody,' Posy pointed out. Maybe a colleague?'

'You don't embrace colleagues the way they were embracing each other.'

'You need to talk to Dulcie about this,' Posy said.

'There were other things, too, things that didn't add up.' A mulish expression crossed Milo's face.

'What sort of things?'

'She's nosy.'

Posy burst into a peal of laughter. 'There's nothing wrong with that.'

'I didn't mention anything before because I know you liked her.'

Privately, Posy felt it was a good thing for Milo to have a taste of his own medicine. He often had several relationships on the go at one time.

'What else did she do?'

'She asked a lot of questions.'

'That's only natural. She admitted she likes finding out about things and she would want to know all about you.'

'Not about me. About you.'

'Me?' Posy dropped her slice of toast.

'And your friend, Iris.'

'We did ask her to investigate Iris's background.' Posy reminded him. 'Are you sure you're not inventing excuses to cool things down between you?'

'I know it sounds silly, but I suspect she was stalking me.'

'Hang on,' Posy cautioned.

'I haven't lost the plot,' Milo insisted. 'She was hanging around the airport concourse for no good reason the day we met and she deliberately bumped into me.'

'So?'

'You don't think that's strange?'

'You're acting like a spoilt child.'

'No, I'm not.'

'You didn't give her a chance to explain and it is early days in your relationship. You've got to take time to get to know each other.'

'If she rings again I'm out,' Milo insisted. 'Finished?' He scooped up Posy's plate. 'You hadn't forgotten it's the railway club meeting tonight?'

'I had, actually,' Posy admitted.

'And it's my turn to be host.'

'I suppose that means they'll all be coming here and playing trains and making a lot of noise until after midnight?'

'We won't disturb you. Sorry, forgot to ask.' Milo turned back from the doorway. 'Any news on Iris?'

'There's still no sign of her.'

'Let me know if I can be of help.'

'Did I tell you Dulcie found out Iris was adopted?'

Milo seemed disinterested by this

piece of information.

'I'm going upstairs to get things ready.' There was a ring at the front doorbell. 'That'll be for me.'

Posy picked up Iris's scarf. She held out little hope that it might provide a clue as to her friend's whereabouts. Whoever had taken it from the kitchen knew of its significance.

They must also have known of Iris's involvement with Anthony Johnson, but why had they put the scarf through his letterbox? It didn't make sense, unless they wanted to warn him of something.

'Hi, Posy.' A railway-club guest poked his head round the kitchen door. 'I found this on the doormat.'

He passed over an envelope covered in muddy footprints.

'Posy?' Milo wheedled from the doorway.

She looked up.

'Do you a trade in exchange for one mended bicycle tyre?'

'What do you want?' She sighed.

'Coffee and eats?'

'And my ankle?'

'You don't have to bring it upstairs. Just text and one of us will come on down.'

After she'd made a mountain of sandwiches and enough coffee and tea to go with them Jena began scratching at the back door.

It was over an hour before Posy remembered her envelope. She looked around the table. It had disappeared.

# Curiouser and Curiouser . . .

Milo was running an iron over his uniform shirt. Steam hissed out of the vents as he applied unnecessary pressure.

'Sorry, no, I haven't seen any envelope.' He frowned, before inspecting his handiwork and hanging the shirt on a hook on the back of the door. 'Run what happened past me again.' He turned his full attention back to Posy.

'One of your friends found an envelope addressed to me on the mat last night and brought it into the kitchen,' Posy repeated her story, 'and now I can't find it.'

'Any idea who it was that found it?'

'I'm not sure but the man who came down to collect the tray of drinks and sandwiches had an Irish accent.'

Milo switched off the iron.

'Irish?' He looked thoughtful. 'I think

his name might have been Liam. Sorry, Posy, I don't have a contact for him.'

'Then where could the envelope have gone?'

'Are you sure it isn't lurking under one of your paintings?'

'Positive.'

'You're welcome to look for it in the studio but don't disturb any settings. Eight by four working models are really challenging. Your friend Liam was very helpful.'

'He's not my friend,' Posy insisted.

'Is that the time? I've gotta go.'

With an armful of shirts Milo paused by the door.

'This envelope wasn't important, was it?'

'If it was from Montague Wilks then probably not.'

'What makes you think it wasn't?'

'He always uses address labels. This envelope was handwritten.'

'Did you recognise the handwriting?'

Posy shook her head.

'Your life's one long mystery at the

moment, isn't it?'

Posy did her best to smile. Milo's jest was too close to the truth to be taken lightly.

*   *   *

'Am I talking to Posy Palmer?' a soft Irish voice enquired as she picked up the telephone later that morning.

'Yes?'

'My name is Liam Dillon. I was at your house last night — the railway club meeting? I was a guest.'

'Of course, I remember you. Did you have a good evening?'

'Sure I did.' There was a pause. 'The reason I'm ringing is because I have something of yours, an envelope. Are you at home now?'

'Yes.'

'Then I'll bring it over if that's all right with you. I can be with you in ten minutes.'

Liam Dillon looked uncomfortable standing on the front doorstep. As well as the envelope, he held a bunch of flowers.

'For me?' Posy gasped in surprise as he handed them to her.

'Thanks for your hospitality last night,' he said. 'I know it must have been disruptive having a house full of men tramping all over the place, prattling on about signal boxes and points failures.'

'Have you time for a cup of tea?' Posy offered out of politeness hoping he wouldn't stay too long. Liam would appear to be a man who talked a lot.

'I've always time for tea.'

Liam ducked as he entered the kitchen.

'It's a lovely place you have here.' He looked around the sunny breakfast bar.

'What can I get you?' Posy asked.

'Builder's tea will be fine, with lots of sugar. Can I make it? You sit down,' he insisted. 'Milo told us about your ankle and I've had plenty of practice at brewing tea. Shall I put these in water to keep fresh?'

He took the flowers from Posy and headed towards the sink.

'Here we are,' he said minutes later. 'One peppermint tea and one builder's.'

Liam pulled out a chair and joined Posy. He looked expectantly at her as if willing her to start up the conversation.

'Your accent . . . ' she began.

'County Westmeath, outside Dublin,' he boasted. 'Have you ever visited that part of the world?'

''Fraid not.

'Any time you want a holiday, let me know.'

'Are you over here on business?' Posy asked when he lapsed into silence.

'Family business.' His smile slipped a little. Underneath his tan Posy detected perspiration on his brow.

'I hope you won't think I'm taking liberties inviting myself over like this,' Liam said, 'but I needed to talk to you.'

'What about?'

'Is your brother around?' Liam cast a glance over his shoulder.

'No.' Posy crossed her fingers under the table so as Liam wouldn't see. 'But I'm expecting him back soon.'

'No matter. It's you I want to talk to.'

Posy's sense of unease returned. Her fingers strayed towards the creased envelope that Liam had placed on the table.

'Best come out with it straight away,' Liam said with a shamefaced smile. Then he took a deep breath. 'I read the contents of your envelope.'

'Do you normally read other people's post?' Posy asked in surprise.

'There's no excuse. It was an accident really. The envelope was unsealed and the sheet of paper fell out. I glanced at it, then once I started reading I had to finish it. It's a letter.'

'Then you can tell me who it's from, can't you?' All the warmth left Posy's voice.

Liam stirred his strong tea.

'First things first. I am here under false pretences,' Liam admitted.

'I think you'd better explain yourself.'

Posy was finding it difficult to restrain her anger.

'You've every right to be annoyed — that's why I wanted to speak to you personally.'

'I'm not sure I want to continue this conversation, Mr Dillon. Thank you for the envelope. If you'll excuse me, I am busy.'

'Please, hear me out. The letter is from your friend, Iris.'

Questions crowded into Posy's head.

'How do you know Iris is a friend of mine?' was the first one she could think of.

'Perhaps you'd better read the letter, what there is of it.'

Liam eased the sheet of paper out of the envelope and passed it to Posy as if he were scared it would disintegrate.

*Dearest Posy,*
*It's a while since we've been in touch but I have kept up to date with your career. I downloaded your app and I know how successful you are,*

*which makes me very proud.*

*My life, too, has changed since we left school. I won't go into details but I have a huge personal problem and I need to talk to someone about it, someone I can trust.*

*After my mother died I married a man called Stephen Fairfax . . .*

Here the letter tailed off as if she had been interrupted. Posy turned the sheet of paper over.

'Where's the rest of it?' she asked.

Liam shrugged.

'That's all there is.'

Posy picked up the envelope, shook it, then studied the letter again.

'Why would anyone want to send me a half-written letter?'

'It's strange to be sure.'

'Well, thank you for passing it on to me.'

Jena stirred in her basket, opened an eye, then went back to sleep.

'Actually, I need to talk to you about Iris.'

'What has she to do with you?' Posy's unease returned.

'I don't know where to start . . . '

'Then perhaps you should save what you have to say for another time.'

'I'm the seventh son of a seventh son,' Liam said with a nervous swallow. 'In folklore that's supposed to be really lucky. In my case it's the reason for what happened to Iris.'

Posy felt in need of back-up and wished Sam would make one of his unscheduled visits.

'Did you know Octavia means the eighth child?'

Posy stared at Liam.

'Are you trying to tell me Iris is your sister?'

'It's possible.'

'And that's why you are here?'

'I have been doing some research into our family tree. If I'm right, I was the child born before Octavia. My mother would talk to me about her when my father was out of the house.

'Money was tight, you see, and there

167

wasn't enough food for eight children. My father insisted that as a seventh son I had to stay with the family even though my mother had always longed for a daughter.'

'After Octavia there were no more children. My brothers were a lot older than me and sometimes I felt like an only child. I often wondered what happened to my baby sister but I couldn't do anything about tracing her while my parents were alive.

'My father wouldn't have her name mentioned and it was only through my mother that I knew I had a sister.

'With the rest of the family grown up I decided to try to find out what happened to her. I'm not married, you see, and I have no other family.'

'How sure are you that Iris is your sister Octavia?'

'Pretty sure.'

'And you told Iris of this? Is that what caused her disappearance?'

'I've never met her.'

'Why should I believe you?'

'It is the truth,' Liam insisted.

'I don't believe in coincidence.'

'I'm not a coincidence.'

'You arrive on the scene the same time as Iris, spouting some story about her being your long-lost sister and then she promptly disappears?'

'Hear me out. I haven't told you everything.'

'You've told me enough.'

'I know I'm not so good at putting words together, that's why I got my second cousin several times removed, actually — to help me.'

'Then good luck with the rest of your research. If you're planning a reunion with Iris I can't help you.'

'I don't know what I was planning.' Liam fiddled with the empty envelope.

'I do. Sam was right all along.'

'Sam?'

'He said follow the money and that's exactly what you've been doing, isn't it?'

Liam paled.

'No.'

'Iris was left a lot of money by her father. Did you demand a share?'

'No.'

'What really happened last night? Did you forge this letter?'

'I haven't forged anything,' Liam insisted.

'Did you hope I'd tell you where Iris is?'

'It was a bad idea to come, wasn't it?' Crestfallen, Liam half stood up.

'You didn't take this letter away by accident last night, did you? You had it with you all the time.'

A guilty look crossed Liam's face.

'I dropped the letter in the hall in error. With so much coming and going I wasn't able to go back for it.

'Then, when I found it on your kitchen table, I didn't want you to read it without having a chance to explain things to you so I slid it under the tea tray when you weren't looking. It took me ages to pluck up the courage to telephone you this morning.'

'I'll say this for you, you know how to

spin a good tale.'

'It's the truth.'

'Then I have some more truths for you, Liam. You're wasting your time. I have no idea what's happened to Iris.' Posy picked up the envelope and inspected it. 'Where did you find this letter?'

'In Iris's room,' Liam confessed.

'You said you'd never met her.'

'The room was empty. The door was open. I think the housekeeper had gone looking for laundry or some such. It was obvious Iris wasn't there.

'That's when I noticed the envelope in the wastepaper bin.'

'How did you know Iris was staying at the Palace?' Posy demanded.

Liam hesitated, looked towards the hall then back to Posy.

'Do you think one of us should answer that?' It was then Posy realised that someone was ringing the front door bell.

# Who to Trust?

Liam came back into the kitchen.

'You've met my second cousin, haven't you? The one I was telling you about.'

'Hello, Posy. I was sorry to hear about your accident.'

Posy stared at a Dulcie who looked far from her usual composed self. Two bright red spots of colour stained her cheeks and her hair wasn't fashioned into its usual sleek bob.

'Dulcie's your what?' Posy asked in a daze.

'The relationship's a bit complicated,' Liam replied. 'Lots of aunties and uncles involved. No need to bother with it right now.'

'Liam told me he wanted to research the family tree.' Dulcie seemed anxious to put her side of the story as quickly as possible. 'I offered to help.'

An eerie silence fell on the kitchen. It was Posy who spoke first.

'I didn't believe Milo when he said you were stalking him, Dulcie, but he was right, wasn't he?'

'No,' Dulcie protested. 'I did bump into him on purpose the day we met but I told you about that.'

'Somehow you found out I knew Iris and you wormed your way into Milo's confidence.'

'That's not what happened.' Dulcie bit her lip. 'Liam, what have you been saying to upset Posy? I've never seen her like this.'

'And Liam.' Posy turned to face him. 'I presume you were the man Milo saw hugging Dulcie in the faculty coffee bar?'

'Milo saw us? Why didn't he speak to me?' Dulcie looked even more distressed.

'Because he thought you were two-timing him,' Posy replied.

Jena whimpered in her basket.

'If you'll excuse me,' Posy stood up,

'I need to take Jena out for a walk. And I'd like you to leave — now,' she added so sharply both Liam and Dulcie jumped.

'If you'd let me explain,' Liam interposed.

'This stops here.' Posy was past listening to either of them. Attaching Jena's lead to her collar she stood up straight. 'Close the front door behind you, please. We are going out the back way.'

Dulcie flushed a deep red.

'It isn't what you think, Posy.' Dulcie made a movement in her direction but Liam restrained her.

'I can see we've outstayed our welcome. Thank you for the tea,' he said, and with his hand under Dulcie's elbow he urged her out of the kitchen.

Jena whined, her tongue warm and comforting as she licked Posy's fingers.

'Come on,' Posy said when her heart had stopped beating like a trip hammer and returned to its normal rhythm. 'We need to get out of here.'

Careful not to put too much strain on her ankle she edged her way across the kitchen with Jena pattering obediently beside her.

An invigorating breeze blew in off the sea as they made their way to the promenade. Posy could see the tide was on the turn as she carefully navigated the walkway that led on to the beach.

Taking off her rope-soled deck shoes she wriggled her toes. Her bare feet sank into the warm gritty sand.

She couldn't stop thinking about Liam and Dulcie. How could they be responsible for Iris's disappearance? Had they spooked her into running away?

Had they heard about her inheritance and wanted a share? Even threatened her?

That didn't make sense. Iris wasn't the running away type and what could they possibly threaten her with? It wasn't news that Iris was adopted anyway why would she be ashamed of adoption?

Then there was the letter. If it were genuine why had Iris broken off halfway through writing it? If she believed Posy was the only one she could trust then why hadn't she kept their date or been in touch?

There was Anthony, too. Who had sent him the silk scarf and why?

'Hello, Posy.'

She felt a hand on her arm.

'This is becoming a habit, bumping into old schoolfriends on the seafront.'

Hannah Clarke was looking even more glamorous than the last time they had met. Her green top was covered with golden stars and her matching lime crops revealed enviably tanned legs. Her manicured toenails peeping through diamanté flops were a delicate shade of peach.

Posy shaded her eyes against the sun.

'You're still here?' was all she could think of to say.

'So it would seem.'

'Why?'

Posy knew she sounded abrupt but she wasn't in the mood for manners.

'My boss is in talks with a potential client. They'll probably go on until midnight if they can't reach an agreement.' Hannah raised her eyes. 'I sneaked away on the pretence of going to the powder room. I don't think anyone noticed me leave.

'I knew I'd go stir crazy if I stayed in that stuffy room for a moment longer. I had to get some air and am I glad I did. Fancy seeing you here.'

'Yes, fancy,' Posy responded in a faint voice, wondering how to tell Hannah she would rather be alone.

'Do you mind if I join you?'

'What about your sandals?'

Posy's experience of working in an office was limited but Hannah's footwear seemed an unusual choice for either a business meeting or a walk along the beach, as did her choice of wardrobe.

'I'll follow your example and take

them off.' Hannah picked up her sandals and dangled them by the straps. 'Ready?'

Jena popped up from behind the breakwater and barked a greeting.

'Hello, little lady. Pleased to see me?'

She threw a pebble in the direction of the water and Jena bolted after it.

'You know, Sealbourne is growing on me.' Hannah took a deep breath. 'It's got a certain quaint charm and can you smell that air? There's nothing like it and I don't mean the whiff of seaweed.' She laughed.

'Have you heard from Iris?'

'You believe in getting right down to business, don't you?' Hannah was still smiling. 'In answer to your question, no, I haven't. Not that I expected to.'

'Do you know Anthony Johnson?' Posy persisted as they plodded along.

'Who's he?' Hannah asked.

'The vicar of All Saints.'

'Isn't that the church in Littlehurst? I think Stephen and I may have visited it that time we stayed over with Iris. Iris used to sing in the choir, didn't she?'

'She now performs with a chamber choir. They did a concert at All Saints a little while ago and she struck up a friendship with Anthony Johnson.'

'Did she indeed?'

The two of them walked on in silence for a few minutes.

'I presume you've been in touch with this Anthony?' Hannah asked. Posy nodded. 'Does he know where Iris is?'

'I don't believe in coincidence,' Posy repeated what she had said to Liam.

'How do you mean?' Hannah asked.

Posy stood square in front of her and ticked them off on her fingers.

'You, Liam and Dulcie. That's three coincidences.'

'Sorry, sweetie, you've lost me there.'

'You all arrive down here at exactly the same time that Iris disappears. You all have a connection with her yet none of you has ever previously visited Sealbourne — why Sealbourne, and why now?'

'I've told you why I'm here. Maybe my visit was a coincidence. They do happen.'

'Once, yes, but not three times.'

'Forgive my ignorance but who are Liam and Dulcie?'

'I'm not sure.'

'Posy, what are you talking about?' Hannah's voice was edged with frustration.

Posy winced as pain stabbed her ankle.

'Then there's my punctured bicycle tyre and the unfinished letter.'

Hannah looked at her in concern.

'You're not running a temperature, are you? Have you overdone the painkillers?'

'Nothing makes sense.'

'There we are in total agreement. Look.' Hannah adopted a conciliatory tone. 'Why don't we get a juice or something at that divine little café over there. We can sit outside where we won't be overheard. I think we have some serious talking to do.'

'That's about it,' Posy said as she finished updating Hannah.

'You're right,' Hannah looked thoughtful, 'there are far too many coincidences for comfort. In my defence I can only say that you were the one who contacted me asking if anyone remembered Iris. I really did bump into her by accident that day we met on the promenade, the same way I bumped into you this afternoon.

'If you don't believe me I guess there's nothing I can do about it, but it's the truth.'

'I didn't mean to doubt your word.' Posy felt ashamed of her earlier outburst.

'I understand. It must have been a shock when Liam knocked on your door. Do you really think he and Dulcie are after Iris's inheritance?'

'Even if they are, why would she run away?'

'Mmm.' Hannah looked thoughtful.

'It doesn't sound like her style.'

'Can you tell me about your brother?' Posy asked carefully.

'Stephen? There isn't much to tell, really. I don't know whether or not he was the great love of Iris's life, but I suppose she was lonely after her parents' deaths and they seemed to get on well enough. Many marriages have been based on less.'

'What happened?'

Hannah eyelids flickered as if the memory was a painful one.

'I mentioned my brother was in the army?' Posy nodded. 'He was based in Germany. He and Iris . . . ' Hannah paused. 'They were going through a trial separation. I think they may have been making plans to get back together but before they could, he died.

'We think he was tired or distracted, maybe thinking about Iris. Whatever, the tyre marks showed that he had skidded and lost control of the car.

'Iris didn't attend the funeral. I suppose I was annoyed that she hadn't made the effort to come with me, if only out of respect for Stephen. Anyway, afterwards things were a little cool between us.

'That's the reason why I was so pleased to reconnect with her. I wanted to let bygones be bygones and I'm sure she felt the same. I can't believe seeing me was anything to do with her disappearance. What possible threat could I pose?'

'Then it's got to be either Liam or Dulcie.'

'Unless Anthony's not all he seems.'

'Anthony?' Posy widened her eyes.

'We've only his word he is who he says. I'm sure he wasn't the incumbent at All Saints when Stephen and I paid our visit.'

'But he knows all about Iris and the concert and her family.'

'That wouldn't be difficult to research.'

'He can't be a fraud. He had the keys to the church.'

'Did you see him open the door?'

'No,' Posy admitted reluctantly.

'Does he have any definite connection to Iris, one you can prove?'

'Only Iris's scarf but I can't see him stealing it from Zephyr Cottage.'

'You're several steps ahead of me again, Posy. A stolen scarf?'

'Did you see it when you had tea with Iris? It's bright scarlet silk and had the initials OL embroidered in the corner.'

'I can't say I remember it. What was it doing in your cottage?'

'Iris left it behind in her hotel room. A waiter gave it to me.'

'And you're saying someone stole it from you?'

'Yes.'

'Your story sounds so fantastic,' Hannah said slowly, 'I'm beginning to believe something serious has happened to Iris.'

'I can't go to the police — but you could,' Posy urged.

'And say what?'

'They'd have to listen to you,' Posy insisted.

'I don't know if my word would carry

much weight. I'm an ex-sister-in-law who hadn't seen Iris for a long time and we weren't even that close. They'd probably tell me to go away and have another look for her.'

'We've got to do something.'

Hannah frowned.

'Why can't you go to the police?' she asked.

'It's history now but I reported someone missing.' Posy reddened at the memory. 'It's a long story but the police accused me of wasting their time.'

'I can see how that could make things awkward for you,' Hannah agreed.

'So?'

Hannah nodded.

'I will go to the police but on the condition that you come with me. You can stay outside, if you like, but I want your support as back-up, safety in numbers and all that. You don't drive, do you? Right, well leave it with me. I'll arrange something.'

Hannah glanced at her bracelet wristwatch.

'Now I really should be getting back before anyone decides to report *me* missing. *Ciao.*'

Posy watched her saunter back across the sand towards the Palace Hotel with her sandals slung over her shoulder. Had she been right to place her trust in Hannah?

Would the police believe her story this time?

# Danger Warning

Sam slapped his steering wheel in frustration. Charcoal clouds scudded across the horizon. The birds had stopped singing. Everywhere was eerily quiet.

He had been a fool to drive out in weather like this. If only he hadn't been so worried about Posy.

If what Anthony had told him was true then Posy was in more danger than either of them had previously realised.

Sam turned the key in the ignition but nothing happened. Grabbing his mobile he looked at the screen in dismay. No signal.

The car rocked from side to side, buffeted by the wind. He took several deep breaths. He didn't remember passing a service station on the way over, so what other options were there?

He needed help but who was there to ask?

Anthony Johnson had proved he couldn't be trusted and as for Liam and Dulcie, Sam had no idea where he stood with them. They seemed genuine but appearances could be deceptive.

Earlier that afternoon a man had crashed into his cubbyhole of an office.

'Sam Barrington?' he had demanded.

\* \* \*

The expression in the man's vivid blue eyes was unsettling.

'What do you want?'

'We're wasting time.'

'I think you'd better leave,' Sam ordered in a calm authoritative voice.

'Please let me in,' a female voice behind him pleaded.

It was only then Sam noticed Dulcie. She pushed her way past her companion with a look of desperation on her face.

'What's this all about?' Sam demanded.

'You've got to help!' Dulcie sounded desperate. 'We didn't mean for any of this to happen.'

'It's no good appealing to his better nature; he doesn't have one.' Her companion sounded disgusted.

'I think,' Sam forced his way into the exchange, 'it might be better if we continued this discussion in a more public. place.'

'Posy's in trouble,' Dulcie blurted out.

'What?' Sam's heart sank.

'Didn't you hear what the lady said?' The man spoke slowly and with a strong Irish accent. 'Posy needs help. Is that clear enough for you?'

Sam continued to stare at Dulcie.

'It was you I saw in the hotel foyer, wasn't it?'

'Do you not understand what we're telling you?' Liam's tone was threatening.

'This has gone far enough,' Sam snapped.

Dulcie moved fractionally towards him.

'Posy's in terrible danger,' she said. 'We've come to you because you're the only person we can turn to. Milo's away and Posy won't talk to us.'

'She threw us out,' Liam put in.

'And I'm about to do the same thing.'

'Why will no-one listen?' Liam screwed up his face in anguish.

Sam hesitated.

'Take it easy.' He made a calming gesture with his hands. 'Start from the beginning.'

'We followed Posy down to the beach,' Dulcie explained.

'That's not the beginning, that's the end.' Liam still sounded upset.

'She was with Hannah Clarke,' Dulcie persisted with her explanation.

'Now do you believe us?' Liam was growing redder in the face.

'How do you know Hannah?' Sam asked.

'You'll have to take our word for it

that we do,' Dulcie replied. 'It's too complicated to explain right now.'

'Right, well what's wrong with Posy and Hannah taking a walk along the beach together? They're old school friends.'

'Hannah's dangerous,' Liam said in a gruff voice.

'You're not suggesting she's going to attack Posy? Tell me exactly what's going on and why you don't trust Hannah.'

'We don't have time!' Liam's colour was still rising.

'Liam is Iris's brother and my second cousin. Tell him, Liam,' Dulcie urged.

'What's the point? I don't seem to be getting through. It's a long story.'

'You've already told me that once so the sooner you get on with it,' Sam interrupted, 'the sooner I'll know what this is all about.'

Dulcie nodded at Liam.

'My mother told me I had a sister, Octavia, who had been adopted by an English couple,' he mumbled, a sulky look on his face before lapsing into silence.

'Go on,' Sam encouraged him.

'After Ma died I wanted to find out what happened to her. I'd always felt there was something missing from my life, the little sister I lost.'

Sam nodded but said nothing.

'I searched on family tree websites for hours. It was more difficult than I thought and I almost gave up.

'Then I had a stroke of luck. There was a piece about a church concert on a secular website. The soloist was listed as Octavia Laxton. She was about the right age.

'I know it was a slim lead but it was the only one I had. Octavia's quite an unusual name and there was a blurry picture of her. I could instantly see the resemblance to my mother. Something told me it was her.'

'Liam asked me to follow it up,' Dulcie said, 'and I found out Octavia Laxton had been married to a man called Stephen Fairfax.'

'Why didn't you tell me any of this earlier?' Sam demanded.

'Let us finish what we've got to say before you start asking questions.' Liam still sounded angry.

'Hannah Clarke contacted us,' Dulcie took up the story. 'She'd read one of Liam's posts saying he was looking for his sister. She told us it was her brother who had been married to Iris. We became convinced we were on the right track.'

'So now you know,' Liam said, 'will you help us?'

'None of this explains why you think Posy is in danger.'

'When I told Hannah I was thinking of coming over to England for a visit, Hannah told me that Iris had been left a substantial sum of money by her father. Then she more or less accused me of being after her inheritance. I tried to persuade her that was the last thing on my mind.'

'To our surprise,' Dulcie cut in, 'she seemed to have a change of heart and said she would contact Iris. She suggested we all meet up at the Palace Hotel and that she would arrange everything.'

'What changed your mind about her?'

'We got here as arranged but neither she nor Iris turned up. Liam tried making enquiries about Iris at the desk but they couldn't help.'

'How did you get involved with Posy and Milo?' Sam asked.

Dulcie flushed a deep shade of pink.

'That was my idea. We were having tea in the lounge and we heard all the fuss going on when Posy arrived for her date with Iris and you accused her of wasting everybody's time.'

'It didn't take Dulcie long to work out something wasn't right,' Liam put in before Sam could object. 'She's clever like that.'

'We would have come over and talked to you,' Dulcie shrugged, 'but you didn't believe Posy so why would you believe us?'

'That's when we decided to go under cover,' Liam explained.

'It wasn't difficult to find out where Posy lived and that she had a brother called Milo who worked for an airline. We decided he would be the perfect go-between so I engineered a meeting.

'We got together and I really liked him, but I think he started to suspect we were up to something. He stopped taking my calls.'

'Dulcie told me Milo was interested in model railways so I attended a club meeting as a guest,' Liam said.

'Why?' Sam asked.

'Liam found an envelope in Iris's room, addressed to Posy with a half-finished letter inside. It seemed important and it was the only clue we had.'

'You held on to it?' Sam demanded.

'I know I shouldn't have taken it but I heard voices in the corridor outside. I think one of them was Posy's. There wasn't time to think. I nipped out before she saw me.'

Liam shrugged.

'I knew things didn't look good. Would you have believed my story? You're not sure I'm telling the truth now, are you?'

Sam had the grace to look shame-faced.

'If something was worrying Iris we thought it was to do with the letter,' Dulcie said, 'but we kept coming up against a brick wall. So we decided to talk to Posy, only it didn't work out as we'd planned.'

'Do you have the letter now?'

'We left it with Posy.'

'What does it say?'

'It was unfinished. Iris said she trusted Posy and that she wanted to talk to her.'

'I seem to have underestimated your abilities,' Sam acknowledged after a short pause.

'Can we talk this through later?' Dulcie began looking anxious again. 'We're wasting precious time.'

'All what you've told me is circumstantial,' Sam pointed out.

'Not that again,' Liam pleaded.

'We're on the level.'

'Why would Hannah want to harm Posy?' Sam asked.

'I don't know but I saw Hannah with Iris's scarlet scarf. How do you explain that?' Dulcie demanded.

'What? When?' Sam fired the question at her with lightning speed.

'I'd taken to hanging around hotel reception in the hopes of catching sight of Iris but instead I saw Hannah. I would have run after her only she was getting into a car and a corner of Iris's scarf was hanging out of her bag.'

'You can't be sure it was the same one,' Sam was quick to point out.

'I know I'm right.'

'Dulcie has an eye for these things,' Liam said quietly, 'and her word is good enough for me. So are you doing to do anything to help us?'

'I need to speak to Anthony Johnson,' Sam said.

'Who?' Liam demanded.

'The vicar of All Saints, Littlehurst. He's a close friend of Iris's.'

'Why do you need to see him?'

'Because he gave Iris the scarf as a present and I think he knows more than he's telling us.'

The background chatter of the kitchen staff preparing trays for afternoon tea was the only sound to break the silence in the office.

'What about Posy?' Dulcie demanded.

'You say you left Hannah and Posy on the beach?'

'The last we saw of them they went into the café.'

'How long ago was this?'

'About an hour?' Liam hazarded a guess.

'Posy will be quite safe, especially if she's got Jena with her.'

Dulcie and Liam looked at each other.

'We have to trust Sam,' Dulcie insisted. 'We have no other choice.'

'Do you want us to come with you to Littlehurst?' Liam asked.

'No, you stay here.'

Sam unhooked his car keys off the wall.

'I'll be back as soon as I can.'

The rain had now begun to abate and Sam opened his car door. If he couldn't get a mobile signal, the only option was to walk.

Sam pressed *redial*.

'Hello?' He heard a muffled voice crackle down the line and the sound of Jena barking in the background.

'Milo? Thank goodness I've got you.'

'You're lucky you did. I'm jet-lagged. I always am after doing a Far East trip. Posy's gone out.'

'Do you know where?'

'Hang on. She left a note on the table.'

There was a moment's silence.

'That's odd.' Milo sounded puzzled.

'What's the matter?'

'Sam, where are you?' Milo asked.

'Stranded on the road from Little-hurst to Sealbourne. My car's broken down.'

'Stay where you are,' Milo ordered. 'I'm coming to fetch you.'

# Love or Money?

'Do you know where Posy's gone?' Sam shouted over the raging wind.

'She didn't say,' Milo shouted back.

Sam gritted his teeth and clung on to the door handle as Milo veered along the country lanes negotiating the hairpin bends at an alarming speed.

'On the phone you said something was strange about Posy's note?' Sam ventured.

'It said she was going out with a friend.'

'And she didn't say where or who?'

'No.'

'So what was odd about it?'

'She signed the note Josephine.'

Baffled Sam stared at Milo.

'And?' he prompted.

'It's our secret signal. She signs off Josephine and I put Miloslav. Mum was going through her Slavic phase when we were born. Lucky she didn't call me Napoleon, I suppose. She liked reading up about the French Revolution, too.'

Milo grinned.

'We looked up the origin of our names one day. Mine means glory and Josephine is someone who loves the arts. I guess Mum got it right with one of us. Josephines can also enhance your life — that describes my sister pretty well, wouldn't you say?'

'Posy signed off as Josephine?' Sam cut across Milo's rambling explanation.

'Didn't I say that?'

'And that's your secret signal?'

'Yes.'

'What does it mean?'

Milo pulled into Zephyr Cottage forecourt.

'It's difficult to explain to someone who isn't a twin.'

'Try,' Sam urged.

'We use it if we want to convey a sub text. Should anyone else read the message they won't see anything unusual in it apart from us signing off with our real names.'

'You think Posy was trying to tell you something that she didn't want anyone else knowing?'

'Posy doesn't get scared but she must have sensed something wasn't right. Let's get inside. It's filthy weather and I'm going to need a gallon of coffee. I've a feeling it's going to be a long night.'

Two figures rushed at them out of the darkness.

'Where have you been?'

Milo froze at the sound of Dulcie's voice.

'What are you doing here?'

She ignored him and went to Sam.

'Liam and I got fed up waiting for you. We decided we had to do something so we came over here, but the place is in darkness.'

'I'm sure I saw someone driving off,' Liam insisted, 'and I thought I heard raised voices but what with the wind and the rain it was difficult to tell.'

'My car broke down,' Sam explained.

'Milo rescued me.'

'Milo.' Dulcie tilted her chin at him, her eyes deep and full of mistrust.

'Who's this?' Milo cast Liam a scathing look.

'I'm Liam — the man you saw hugging Dulcie.' Liam's voice reflected the mistrust in Dulcie's eyes.

'Look, can we save this until later?' Sam demanded.

'Did you speak to Anthony? Does he know anything about Hannah? Has he heard from Iris? Where's Posy?' Dulcie bombarded Sam with questions.

Liam restrained her.

'Sure, aren't we all looking like drowned rats? Let's get inside.'

'You don't have to stay.' Milo barged past Liam.

'Come on.' Sam ushered everyone into the kitchen.

I'll make the tea,' Liam insisted.

'Coffee for me.' Milo stripped off his saturated jumper and draped it over the clothes airer.

'Is this the note?' Sam snatched it up

off the table and scanned the contents.

'See?' Milo peered over his shoulder.' All Posy says is she's going out with a friend.'

'What's that?' Liam tried to grab the note.

'Josephine.' Dulcie peered over Sam's other shoulder and read the signature aloud.

'She only signs with her real name when she wants to tell me something but she doesn't want anyone else to know,' Milo explained.

'For goodness' sake, man, you're not a mind reader. How in the blazes are you supposed to know what's going on?' Liam demanded.

'And who's she out with?' Dulcie added.

'Posy doesn't drive. She wasn't with you, Milo. It has to be Hannah I heard driving off,' Liam said slowly and carefully. 'But who was doing all the shouting?'

'And where were they going?' Dulcie screwed up her face. 'If only Posy had left another clue.'

'Did you find out anything from Anthony?' Liam placed three mugs of tea on the table, together with a pot of coffee.

'Here, drink this.' He poured some out for Milo. 'You're the one who knows your sister best. We need you to stay awake.'

'Remind me, who's Anthony?' Milo ignored Liam.

Sam picked up one of the mugs of tea.

'He and Iris are friends,' Dulcie explained. 'Sam thought he was holding out on us so he drove over to see him.'

'And was he?' Milo asked. 'Holding out on you?'

'You could say that.' Sam looked round the table. 'Anthony and Iris are married.'

'What?' Dulcie's mouth dropped open with shock.

'When?' Liam demanded.

'A month ago.'

'Then why on earth hasn't he been

out there scouring the streets looking for her with the rest of us?' Liam demanded.

'Because she asked him not to.'

'You're not serious?'

'It seems she said she would be in touch and that he wasn't to worry if he didn't hear from her for a while. She said she had something important she had to sort out,' Sam replied.

'And Anthony accepted that?' Milo asked.

'Seems so, until he received Iris's silk scarf.'

'Hey!' Milo banged his mug of coffee down on the table. 'Wasn't that the one we had here?'

'And it disappeared the night Posy's bicycle tyre suffered a puncture,' Sam replied.

'I don't believe Hannah broke in and stole a scarf.' Milo shook his head.

'She didn't have to break in,' Sam pointed out. 'Posy left the back door unlocked.'

'I'm always telling her about that, but

she never listens to me.' Milo sounded annoyed. 'She gets busy with her painting and everything practical goes out of her mind.'

'Hold on a moment.' Dulcie held up her hand. 'I have some questions.'

'I'd like some answers, too,' Liam agreed.

'I don't have all the answers,' Sam said.

'Then tell us what you do know,' Liam insisted, 'before we all go mad trying to work it out for ourselves.'

'Iris made an appointment to meet up with Posy which she didn't keep.'

'That's old news,' Milo interrupted.

'Posy found a card in Iris's wastepaper basket with the name Stephen Fairfax on it.'

'And we know Stephen was Iris's first husband,' Liam agreed.

'Was the half-finished letter you found in Iris's room also in the wastepaper bin?'

'It was,' Liam replied.

'Then I think Stephen Fairfax's card

was probably in the same envelope and it fell out.'

'But why didn't Iris finish the letter?'

'I said I didn't have all the answers.'

'Go on,' Milo urged Sam.

'I think in her hurry to leave the hotel Iris left her scarf behind.'

'Agreed,' Liam nodded.

'I don't know who you are,' Milo interrupted, 'but this is nothing to do with you, so why don't you butt out?'

'It's everything to do with Liam,' Dulcie said.

'Or you, either, so why don't you take your boyfriend back to wherever it is you came from and leave me and Sam to sort things out?'

'Boyfriend, is it?' A slow smile spread across Liam's face. 'I'll have you know I'm Iris's brother.'

'He's also my second cousin. I'll explain later, now stop interrupting and let Sam get on with his story.'

Dulcie's expression softened a fraction.

'You weren't jealous of Liam, were you?'

'Course he was,' Liam pronounced with a wry smile. 'Look, he's gone red in the face.'

'What's all this about you being Iris's brother?' Milo demanded.

'Can we get back to Posy?' Sam raised his voice.

'Sorry, go on about the scarf,' Dulcie turned her attention back to Sam.

'I'm guessing this bit,' Sam explained, 'but I think Hannah found the cottage door open. Posy wasn't here but the scarf was.'

'And she took it?'

'Yes.'

'Why?'

Liam sat up straight.

'I know — she wanted Anthony to think Iris was with her.'

'I'm still confused,' Dulcie said.

'I think Hannah tried to blackmail Iris. When she disappeared Hannah turned her sights on Anthony, hoping to blackmail him.'

'That would mean she knew about his marriage to Iris.' Milo looked thoughtful.

'Anthony hasn't got any money,' Dulcie pointed out.

'But he has got a wife,' Sam said.

'I'm getting it,' Liam said. 'Hannah told Iris that Stephen was still alive?'

'How would Anthony's parishioners feel about bigamy?' Sam asked.

'Some of them might not like it,' Liam mused.

'But it wasn't Anthony's fault,' Dulcie pointed out, 'and he still couldn't pay any ransom demand. It was Iris's money, not his.'

'Iris and Anthony are setting up a charity foundation. Anthony had access to the funds.'

'Did Hannah make a ransom demand?'

'He says not. All he received was the scarf.'

'If Stephen is still alive why didn't he visit Sealbourne with Hannah?' Liam asked.

'Because Hannah may have invented

the whole thing.'

'You're beginning to lose me,' Milo said, pouring out a second mug of coffee.

'Didn't someone say blackmail usually involves money or matters of the heart?' Liam spoke slowly.

'Go on,' Sam urged.

'We know Hannah likes the good things in life. Maybe she wanted a slice of Iris's inheritance.

'What could be easier for her than to convince Iris that Stephen was still alive and that her silence on the matter would come at a price?'

'But that's horrible,' Dulcie said.

'Surely Iris could prove her first husband was dead, couldn't she?' Milo asked.

'She could — but Anthony told me they were separated at the time of his death and if he died abroad it would create more problems,' Sam replied.

'None of this explains why Iris disappeared,' Milo said.

'Or why she wanted to see Posy in

the first place,' Dulcie added.

'I think Iris felt that with Posy coming from a bohemian background,' Sam cast an apologetic look at Milo, 'she would be less shocked by Iris's revelation and she probably wanted to ask her what to do.'

'But why didn't Iris wait around for Posy to visit?'

'Probably because Hannah was very convincing. She may have scared Iris into thinking that the authorities were after her. She had to prove Stephen was dead. You were in contact with Hannah, weren't you, Liam?'

'We both were,' Dulcie agreed.

'But you hadn't been in touch with Iris?'

They shook their heads.

'Hannah arranged everything.'

'Then Hannah may have used your names and said you would be calling soon for an informal interview with Iris.'

'So when she learned we had checked in to the hotel she panicked?'

'The poor mite.' Liam paled. 'What an awful thing to do.'

'I'd like to get my hands on Hannah Clarke,' Dulcie said.

'Wouldn't we all?' Liam agreed.

Milo knocked his knee against the table spilling some coffee.

'Even if we are right none of this tells us where Posy has gone and what's worrying her.'

'My guess is that Posy was making too much noise about Iris's disappearance,' Sam said.

'You don't mean Hannah's going to silence her?' Milo sprang to his feet. 'We have to go after them.'

'Yes — but where have they gone?' Dulcie's voice rose in panic.

'They could be anywhere,' Liam agreed.

'I know where they went,' a voice interrupted from the doorway.

# Terror on the Cliffs

Milo's chair crashed to the floor as he stepped back in surprise. The sound reverberated around the kitchen, causing Jena to bark and run round in circles.

'Who are you?' he demanded.

The woman's red hair was plastered to her head. Raindrops dripped off her fringe and trickled down her cheeks. Her chest rose and fell as she fought to catch her breath.

'Do you have to ask?' Liam's question was in soft contrast to the harshness of Milo's voice.

'Whoever you are, you're soaking wet,' Dulcie sympathised. 'Come and sit down in the warm.'

Making soothing noises she ushered the woman towards the Aga, shooing Jena out of the way.

'Thank you.' The woman sank gratefully into one of the wooden chairs, her teeth chattering.

Dulcie massaged her hands.

'You're frozen. What have you been doing?'

'I'd say she's been running for her life,' Sam said slowly.

'It's Iris, isn't it?' Liam spoke as if addressing a child.

'I'm so sorry,' she whispered.

Dulcie continued to comfort her.

'Thank goodness you're safe.'

Gently releasing her hold on Iris's hands she looked into the trembling blue eyes that were a startling reflection of Liam's.

'You're exactly like Liam,' she said.

'It's like looking into my mother's eyes,' he said in a husky voice.

'Liam?' Iris queried in a shaky voice.

'She's referring to me.' He stepped forward. 'Liam Dillon.'

'And I'm Dulcie Lee.'

The look of panic returned to her face.

'You're here to arrest me for bigamy, aren't you?'

'Indeed I am not,' Liam protested.

'You're not the police?'

'I am not, nor ever have been, involved with police.' Liam looked affronted.

'And you're not from the authorities?'

'We are not,' Dulcie replied, gesturing at Liam to keep back. The expression on Iris's face suggested it wouldn't take much for her to flee out of the door.

'Then what were you doing at the hotel?'

'Let's save that story for another day,' Dulcie said in a soothing voice.

'Here, drink this.' Milo poured out some coffee. 'It'll warm you up.'

Dulcie cupped Iris's hands around the mug and, smiling encouragingly, waited until Iris had taken several sips.

'Welcome to the family.' Liam could keep quiet no longer.

'The family?' Iris repeated in a daze.

'You're a Dillon and I'm your long-lost brother,' Liam announced.

Iris gulped, her eyes watering.

'Really?' She trembled.

'Really,' Liam replied, almost as lost for words.

'And I'm your second cousin,' Dulcie said. 'I'm that pleased to meet you.'

'You know,' Liam interrupted, 'you've caused an awful lot of trouble, Octavia.'

Dulcie relieved Iris of her mug.

'Not now, Liam. Take no notice of Liam's nonsense. You're not in trouble and Liam's as thrilled as I am to meet you. He's spent ages looking for you.'

'As have all of us,' Milo reminded Dulcie, 'but for a different reason.'

'I'm not a bigamist,' Iris spoke quickly, 'and I've got the papers to prove it.'

'Explanations can wait,' Sam insisted.

'You work at the Palace Hotel, don't you?' Iris asked.

'I'm Head of Security,' he replied.

Another look of alarm crossed Iris's face.

'Is this to do with Posy? She's in trouble, isn't she?'

Dulcie winced as Iris dug her fingernails into her arm and cast Milo a pleading look.

'Can you tell us what you know?' Milo coaxed.

'I should have realised Posy wouldn't let things rest when I didn't meet up with her as arranged.'

'She didn't,' Milo agreed. 'I'm Posy's twin brother, by the way.'

Iris blinked at him.

'Posy and I were at school with Hannah Clarke,' she blurted out.

'What do you know about Hannah?' Sam demanded.

Iris screwed up her face in distress.

'We have to get Posy away from her.'

'Then they are together?' Sam demanded in an urgent voice.

Iris nodded.

'I saw them.'

'You said you knew where they'd gone.'

'To the cliff tops.'

'Posy wouldn't go up there,' Milo was adamant, 'not after dark and certainly not in the middle of a storm.'

'Hannah was here, in the kitchen, with Posy,' Iris interrupted him. 'The door was open. I heard their raised voices. They were arguing about going to the police.'

'And you didn't think to make your presence known?' It was Liam's turn to fire a question at Iris.

'I was going to but Anthony rang, I had to speak to him. I wanted to reassure him that I would soon be home. The signal was so bad and I could hardly hear what he was saying above the thunder.

'I moved away from the door to take the call and by the time I'd finished Hannah and Posy were getting into Hannah's car.

'They didn't see me but they were still arguing. I could hear Posy saying she wanted to go to the police but they drove off in the opposite direction.

'I ran after them all the way down to the traffic lights bellowing and shouting but Hannah didn't stop. The lights were green and she took off in the direction of the cliff road.'

Iris was breathing heavily again as she finished her explanation.

'So it was you I heard shouting?' Liam said.

'There's not a moment to lose. We have to go after them,' Sam insisted.

'You don't think Hannah's going to push Posy off the edge?' Dulcie's face was now pale with shocked disbelief.

'I don't know what I think, but the cliffs tops aren't safe and this storm will make things worse.'

'How are we going to get up there?' Milo asked.

'I'll have to borrow your car.' Sam held out his hand for Milo's keys.

'I'm coming with you,' Iris insisted.

'You're in no fit state to go anywhere,' Liam forestalled her.

'I owe it to Posy.'

'Then go,' Milo urged. 'We haven't time to argue the point. This is my sister's life we're talking about.'

Grabbing Jena's collar to hold her

back, he opened the door.

'What on earth is going on? That dog is making enough noise to wake the whole of Sealbourne.'

'Montague,' Milo greeted him.

'Good evening,' he said.

Iris and Sam pushed him into the wall as they rushed outside.

'Manners,' he said, looking after them. 'Really.'

'Can we borrow your car?'

'No, you cannot.' He looked affronted by the idea. 'It's high performance and I don't want you racketing around the countryside. Have you seen what the weather's doing out there?'

'It's an emergency and it involves Posy.'

'What's she done now?' Montague asked on a sigh.

'If you don't help us, your precious exhibition will be written off and you'll lose an awful lot of money.'

'In that case,' Montague replied, 'I might be persuaded to part with my vehicle for a short while.'

'Why don't I stay here and keep you company?' Dulcie stepped in, delivering her most winning smile and batting her eyelashes at him. 'I'd love to hear all about your art work,' she gushed. 'I am such a fan of surrealism.'

'Do you indeed?' Montague, his attention diverted, beamed at her.

He hardly noticed Liam and Milo run out the door in pursuit of Iris and Sam.

'At last — someone intelligent I can talk to.'

The streetlights cast an orange glow on the slippery pavements. The rain had abated but puddles flooded the road forcing Milo to zigzag around the worst of the floods.

'You're not flying one of your aeroplanes now,' Liam cautioned.

'We have to rescue Posy and we're running out of time.'

The rear lights of Milo's car being driven by Sam disappeared into the distance.

'I can't see a wretched thing.'

'They went that way.' Liam pointed to where Sam's rear lights disappeared into the heavy mist signalling the turn off for the cliff road. The mist grew thicker.

'Where on earth are we? I've lost all sense of direction.'

'Over there.' Liam pointed towards a flash of reflector light before it was swallowed up in the deepening gloom.

Milo gripped the steering wheel, his nose inches from the windscreen.

'Would you slow up a moment?' Liam kept his voice steady.

'Why?'

Liam wound down his window and leaned out.

'Because I think they've come to a halt in front of us. Take it steady,' Liam advised as Milo edged forward, 'we don't want us going over the edge.'

'I recognise that bench.' Milo bumped off the rocky road on to soft grass that squelched and sank beneath their tyres. 'This is the viewing area.

There's a shack nearby. It's used by hikers and the wardens who patrol the area.'

Milo leaped out of the car.

'Wait for me,' Liam called after him.

'Hey!' Milo cupped his hand and called into the darkness. 'Where are you?'

'Over here,' Sam's voice echoed back.

'I can't see you.'

The wind whipped Milo's voice away.

Liam tugged his sleeve.

'Stick with me. I'm the expert when it comes to mists.'

'Watch where you're going,' Sam shouted as a few moments later Liam bumped into him.

'I can't see Iris,' he bellowed.

Sam swung round.

'She was here a moment ago.'

'Octavia!' Liam's strong voice rose above the wind. 'Come back here at once!'

The mist continued to swirl around them.

'She's that wound up.' Milo broke

the silence. 'I don't know that she's going to take any notice of you.'

'She'd better. I haven't come all this way to lose her now.'

'She can't have gone far,' Sam said.

'There's a torch in the car,' Milo said.

Sam retrieved it then swung the beam round the deserted viewing area.

'Quiet, everyone,' he cautioned.

Below them the storm-tossed sea battered the rocks. In the distance a siren wailed.

'It's like the end of the world up here,' Liam said in a low voice.

'There's no-one else about. Iris got it wrong,' Milo said.

'What's that?' Sam pointed.

'Where do you mean?'

'Over there.'

'It's them,' Liam pointed to the faint outline of three silhouettes in the distance. 'What the blazes are they doing?'

'They're on the edge of the cliffs.'

'Someone's shouting.'

'Faster, man, or we'll never get there in time.' Milo made to rush past Liam.

'Yes, we will,' Sam insisted. 'But keep the noise down and no sudden movements, we don't want anyone getting the jitters.'

Liam barged forward to the front of the group and Sam grabbed out at him at the same moment as a small blurred shape sped past them.

'What was that?' Milo stepped backwards nearly losing his balance.

Jena barked and raced towards the cliff edge.

'I thought you left her in the kitchen,' Sam shouted above the raging wind, his feet now beginning to pound the sodden turf.

'She must have sneaked into the car,' Milo gasped. 'Get after her.'

'Posy!' Sam's shout was followed by a high-pitched shriek before one of the silhouettes disappeared over the edge.

# Awkward Suggestion

'How does it feel to be a success?'

They were surrounded by the murmur of voices praising Montague and Posy's exhibition. Posy looked paler than usual. She did her best to smile at Sam.

'I'll be glad when it's all over,' she admitted. 'Being the centre of attention isn't my scene.'

'There are dark circles under your eyes.' Sam looked concerned. 'You need to rest up.'

'I will,' Posy promised.

'I suppose you've got to stay?'

'You suppose right.' Posy acknowledged Sam's comment with a weary smile.

'You deserve some down time after all that's happened.' Sam moved in closer to avoid being overheard. Posy could feel his warm breath on her ear.

'Surely Montague realises that?'

'Montague has been a life saver. It was his slave-driving that kept me going. If I hadn't had my work then I would have cracked up,' Posy insisted, wondering why she had ever thought of Sam as unfeeling.

Ever since the accident Sam had been a tower of strength dealing with the authorities, who seemed determined to put the blame for what happened on anyone but themselves.

Sam had taken them to task over inadequate security and not enough safeguards to protect the public from losing their footing on the cliff tops.

The volunteer wardens had taken his side when things had looked like turning nasty and all charges had been dropped with the promise of improved measures to be taken with immediate effect.

'Ms Palmer.' A photographer approached. 'If you wouldn't mind?'

'I'll catch up with you later.' Sam raised his glass to her and wandered off to look at Posy's 'Blue Clocks Waiting For Sunrise'.

'I don't know how she does it.' Milo was standing in front of the centrepiece. 'The artistic gene passed me by. But it is very vibrant,' he added loyally, 'with good use of colour.'

Now reconciled with Dulcie, he had his arm around her shoulder. She looked exquisite in a maroon cocktail dress that showed off her slender figure to perfection.

'Who's that woman having an animated discussion with Posy?' Dulcie peered over Milo's shoulder at the sound of raised voices.

'Where? Good heavens!' The colour had drained from Milo's face.

'What's the matter?'

'It's my mother. The evening could be wrecked if we don't put a stop to them. Fasten your seat belt, Dulcie, and stand by for take off. Vera takes a little getting used to.'

'You call your mother by her first name?'

'Don't ask,' Milo cautioned.

'Want me to tag along?' Sam volunteered.

'Welcome aboard. Vera loves an audience.'

Milo crossed the room and tapped his mother on the shoulder.

'Darling!' Her face lit up and she kissed him on the cheek. 'My, how you've grown. You're so handsome I would hardly recognise you. And who's this?'

Sam tugged at Posy's arm.

'Come on,' he urged as Milo introduced Vera to Dulcie.

'What are you doing?' Posy demanded, trying to shake him off.

'Getting you out of here.'

'I was pointing out the merits of my work to my mother.'

'I heard you and so did most of the room.'

Posy's colour was now heightened and her cheeks flushed.

'Vera doesn't understand what inspires me. I was trying to get through to her.'

'Save it for another time,' Sam suggested. 'Montague won't miss us. Look, he's busy chatting up the movers and shakers. We can safely leave him to that side of things. It's what he does well.'

Posy hesitated, a look of indecision replacing her earlier stubbornness.

'You've been on your feet all day.' Sam pushed home his advantage. 'And you've given masses of interviews. It's time to ease up.'

'We have to say goodbye to Montague and if he says I have to stay then I stay.'

'Come on, then.'

'Have you seen the number of red dots on the canvases?' Montague was bursting with importance. 'Indicating sold, and to very influential people. Your work will be internationally showcased, Posy. You, dear girl, are a hit. Didn't I always say so?'

'Not in so many words,' Posy reminded him.

'Artists!' Montague raised his eyes at

Sam. 'Have nothing to do with them.'

'I'll bear your advice in mind.' Sam smiled.

'Were you the young man who made a mess of my car?' Montague peered at Sam's name badge. 'I have never seen so much mud. The car wash almost gave up the challenge.'

'It wasn't Sam, it was Milo,' Posy put in, 'and we'd like to pay for any damage.'

Montague looked from one to the other.

'No matter.' He gave an airy wave of his hand and then gave way to an unusual display of emotion. 'When I thought something had happened to you . . . Don't do that to me again, will you?'

'I promise,' Posy soothed.

He blinked rapidly and took several deep breaths.

'When Dulcie explained what had been going on I couldn't believe it. I mean here in Sealbourne! It's always been such a respectable place.'

'It's all over now, Montague,' Posy consoled him. 'Why don't you get back to the party?' she suggested.

Montague brightened up.

'I supposed I should. The media are out in force tonight.'

Sam seized his chance.

'Would it be all right if Posy and I made an early night of it, Montague? She's dead on her feet.'

'Anything you like, dear boy,' Montague readily agreed. 'Right now Posy could ask for the moon and I'd do my best to get it for her.' After air-kissing Posy's left ear, Montague turned to Sam.

'Take good care of her for me, Sam, she's a brand now.'

'He's having the time of his life.' Sam smiled as Montague bustled away. 'Do you fancy a nightcap?' he asked.

'We can't go back to Zephyr Cottage.' Posy retrieved her pashmina and wrapped it around her shoulders.

'You needn't worry about the door-stepping nosy parkers. They've moved on.'

'It's my mother,' Posy admitted. 'I'd rather she was safely in bed before I went home. When it comes to art she never knows when to stop.'

'A trait her daughter appears to have inherited.'

'You know I'm too dead beat to argue with you,' Posy admitted.

'Well, I know a quiet nook in the hotel where we won't be disturbed. Come on.'

Posy allowed Sam to hurry her out into the night air.

'Shall we walk?' he asked.

Posy linked her arm through Sam's.

'It's a lovely evening. It's nice to do something as normal as taking a walk.'

They strolled along without speaking for a few moments.

'I don't think I've thanked you,' Posy said in a quiet voice.

Sam put his hand over hers.

'Not necessary.'

'I hate to admit it but you were right all along.'

'Was I?'

'Follow the money.'

They reached the Palace Hotel and Posy paused in the foyer as Iris and Liam emerged from the lift.

'Posy!' Iris ran across the carpet and wrapped her arms around her. 'I wanted to say goodbye but there were so many people we didn't have the chance.'

'You're leaving?'

Posy disentangled herself from Iris and looked from her to Liam.

'We are,' Liam acknowledged. 'My sister has very kindly invited me to stay over with her for a few days.'

'Anthony's gone to fetch the car. Your exhibition was fantastic.' She nudged Liam in the ribs. 'Wasn't it?' she said pointedly.

'Sure it was,' he agreed. 'Posy, we're very proud of you. I can't wait to I get back home and tell everyone I actually know Posy Palmer.'

'I never knew I had such a famous friend.' Iris's face was wreathed in smiles.

Posy had never seen her look so happy. 'Promise we'll keep in touch with each other this time?'

'As long as you don't break any more dates.'

Iris looked a different person from the one who had gatecrashed the cottage a week earlier. She laughed and squeezed Posy's arm.

'I was pathetic, wasn't I? Running off like a frightened schoolgirl, but I couldn't talk to Anthony. That's when I thought of you.'

'Nothing ever shocked the school rebel?' Posy joked.

'When Hannah said Stephen was still alive and that she'd tell Anthony I was a bigamist unless I paid up, I gave it my best shot. I called her bluff and said I didn't believe her. Then I learned a man had been asking about me at hotel reception. I assumed she'd been telling the truth and that it was either Stephen or the authorities.'

'Trust me to be in the wrong place at the wrong time,' Liam joked.

'From now on,' Iris insisted, 'your place is with me.'

'You need looking after, that's for sure, but that's Anthony's job, not mine. But I'm happy to be his second-in-command.' He paused. 'Are you going to tell them the latest development?'

'There's nothing wrong, is there?' Posy cast an anxious look at Sam.

'It's early nights for me from now on and no parties for a while,' Iris said. 'Do you know, I think that's why I acted out of character running away like that? My emotions have been all over the place since I found out.'

'Iris — Octavia,' Liam said in a patient voice, 'put the pair of them out of their misery.'

'Anthony's thrilled to bits. That's him now,' Iris responded to a loud hoot of a car horn in the road outside. 'Come on, Liam, home time.'

Liam gathered up his suitcase and Iris's dropped gloves.

'What she's trying to say, in case you

haven't already guessed, is that I am going to be an uncle.'

Iris turned back to face them.

'You and Sam should try marriage and parenthood some time. Don't look at me like that, Posy, haven't I always known what's best for you?'

'Stop interfering,' Liam chided. 'You're not head girl now. Posy can make her own decisions.'

Iris snorted.

'I've known Posy since she was the school rebel. I was the first to recognise her talent. That fool of an art teacher certainly didn't.'

Anthony strode into the foyer.

'Come on, you two,' he bellowed, his presence dominating the small group. 'I'm on a double yellow line. A friendly warden has given me one minute to move on. Has Iris told you our good news?' He sighted Posy and beamed at her.

'She has and congratulations.'

'I'll ring you next week,' Iris called over her shoulder as Anthony and Liam hustled her out of the foyer.

'Now I know why you had to go looking for her.' Sam smiled as the foyer returned to normal after their departure. 'She's quite some lady.'

'She's the best,' Posy said simply, reluctant to look him in the eye.

She wished Iris hadn't made that remark about herself and Sam. Whilst her feelings towards him had changed, she knew he would always think of her as a rebel, the one who had been accused of wasting police time.

'Let's find this quiet nook of yours,' she said.

\* \* \*

'Peppermint tea or something stronger?' Sam asked as Posy sank into a secluded wing-backed armchair.

'Tea, please, and some strawberry tarts?'

'I'll see what I can do.'

Posy leaned back in her chair with a sigh and closed her eyes, not sure her life would ever be the same again.

She'd read that a person's life flashed before their eyes when they were drowning. Her life had certainly flashed before hers that night on the cliff tops when Hannah had threatened to jump.

'This is all Iris's fault.' She had made a dramatic stand on the edge of the cliffs.

'What did Iris ever do to you?' Posy had shrieked into the night wind, knowing how important it was to keep Hannah talking.

'She inherited a fortune. A slice of it should have been mine. If Stephen hadn't died it would have been. Why did you and that meddlesome Irishman interfere?'

Posy realised Hannah was past listening to reason.

'There's going to be a terrible accident. I tried to save you but you slipped out of my grasp.'

It was then Posy realised Hannah's true intention. She wasn't the one going to jump. She was going to push Posy over the edge.

'No-one will believe you.'

'Yes, they will.'

'Why would we be up here on a night like this?'

'Therapy,' Hannah screeched back at her. 'I was helping you come to terms with your phobia. Everyone knows how scared you are up here.'

Posy swayed. Her senses were slipping away from her. It was only after Hannah took the cliff road and told her that she never had any intention of going to the police that Posy knew her fears had been well founded.

'Posy!'

Posy shook her head. She was hearing things. Iris couldn't be coming to her rescue.

'Let's go back,' Posy pleaded.

'Posy!' The call came again out of the mist and rain.

'Iris, is that you?' she called back.

'I'm not falling for that one,' Hannah

sneered. 'She's not here to help you. No one is.'

Hannah's eyes widened in shock as a blurred figure flew at them out of the mist. A barking Jena launched herself at Posy and a flashing torchlight arced the sky.

Wrong-footed, Hannah lost her balance. Clutching Jena, Posy reached out but she had been too late to grab Hannah's flailing hand.

# Love is in the Air

'Tea's on its way.'

Posy opened her eyes. Sam was standing in front of her. She knew it was no good denying her feelings any longer. Iris had seen what she had been determinedly ignoring. She was in love with Sam.

She didn't know when or how it had happened. She was so used to squabbling with him she had felt quite unprepared for her rush of adrenaline when Sam had climbed down the ledge to where Hannah had fallen and tended to her until the air ambulance arrived. Posy still felt sick at the thought of what might have happened had he too lost his footing.

Posy pulled herself together. Daydreaming about her feelings for Sam was not going to get her anywhere.

'Do you think they'll arrest Hannah?'

'The latest report is that she's suffering nothing more than shock and a broken leg. You don't want to press charges?'

'I'm with Iris on that one. She wants to put the whole thing behind us.'

'Then I doubt things will be taken any further. It would be a difficult case to prove, anyway,' Sam agreed. 'A lot of what happened is hearsay.'

'Hannah confessed in the car. She said we were going up to the cliffs and not to the police station because she couldn't live with what she'd done. She jumped out of the car and ran towards the cliff edge. I had to run after her, but when we got there I froze.'

'Don't ever do anything like that again,' Sam said in a quiet voice.

'How was I supposed to stop Hannah? It all came out — how she'd stolen Iris's scarf from my kitchen and posted it through Anthony's letterbox to scare him into doing something.

'She said I was asking too many questions and Liam and Dulcie were getting suspicious. I think she lost it when I suggested going to the police. Then she started behaving oddly in the kitchen and I knew something wasn't right. That's why I signed my note Josephine.'

'It was as well you did.'

'I hoped Milo would pick it up.'

'He was the hero of the hour, rescuing me, then realising you were in trouble.'

'I agree, but don't tell him — my brother's vain enough as it is.'

'Poor Liam,' Sam said. 'If he hadn't started looking for his long lost sister none of this might have happened. Did Iris say why she didn't finish the letter she was writing to you?'

'She realised, too late, that she didn't want me involved.'

'And the card with Stephen's name on it? How did that come about?'

'Hannah, I think. That's when Iris decided to fly off to Germany, to check up with the authorities on what had happened to Stephen. I don't know how Hannah thought she could get away with pretending he was still alive.'

'Why didn't Iris get in touch with anyone instead of flying off without a word?'

Posy shrugged.

'She told us she wasn't thinking straight. What's going to happen to Hannah?'

'She'll probably be offered professional help. She seems to have been living in a fantasy world. The hotel records show she was down here on her own.'

'There was no workaholic boss?'

'She was unemployed. I suppose that's why she wanted a share of Iris's money. I can tell you she wasn't responsible for your punctured tyre. There were several reports of vandalism in the area that night, but none of it was to do with Hannah. She was busy stealing your scarf.'

'At least Dulcie and Milo are reconciled,' Posy said, 'and Iris and Anthony are going ahead with their plans to set up a charity foundation for performing arts.'

'Everyone's sorted,' Sam smiled. 'And you've a glittering career ahead of you.'

'And you?' Posy asked.

'I have plans,' was Sam's guarded reply.

They were interrupted by the arrival of a waitress bringing a loaded tea tray.

'I went for the full works.' Sam grinned. 'Tuck in.'

Needing no further invitation Posy piled up her plate with a selection of sandwiches.

Finishing her third cup of peppermint tea she folded her napkin neatly at the side of her plate and leaned back in her armchair. She wished she could fall asleep where she was but Sam looked as though he had something on his mind.

'You're not going to go to sleep on me, are you?' he asked.

'Of course not.' She sat up straight.

'Good, because there's never going to be a right moment to do this.'

'To do what?' she queried.

'Talk.'

Posy's heart sank. Whatever Sam had to say she suspected she wouldn't like it.

'You're not going to deliver another lecture on my lifestyle?'

'It's about Maureen, actually.'

Posy didn't want to talk about Sam's wife but before she could say anything Sam began speaking again.

'She didn't like me being in the police force. Being a trained nurse she was used to the unsocial hours and disrupted schedules. What worried her was the thought I might be injured in the course of my duty but,' he shrugged, 'we both knew the risks.'

Posy nodded.

'We'd booked a skiing holiday and we were looking forward to the break, but all police leave was cancelled at short notice the day before we were due to travel. Maureen decided to go on ahead without me. There was an accident. The coach skidded on an icy mountain road.'

Sam bowed his head. Posy leaned forward and placed her hand over his.

'Don't go on.'

He looked up at her.

'You had to know.'

'Why?'

'Because the time has come for me to make a new start in life.'

'You're leaving Sealbourne?'

'I meant my personal life.'

'I'm not sure I understand.' Posy frowned.

'I've decided to move out of the hotel. Living on top of the shop, you never get away from work and that's not a mistake I intend to make again.

'I've got my eye on a property about three miles away. It's small and needs a lot of work doing to it.

'There's an old-fashioned coach house adjacent to the cottage. It's huge and would be an ideal garage and workshop. I've always fancied buying an old car and doing it up.'

'That sounds ideal.' Some of the

249

tension left the back of Posy's neck.

'There's a studio that runs above the whole length of the coach house. It's completely independent with its own water supply and other facilities.

'It's got a sunshine roof that can be opened and closed depending on the weather.'

'How lovely.' Still mystified, Posy waited for Sam to go on.

'You like the idea?'

'I do.'

'You don't think I'm an unfeeling brute with no heart who doesn't have an artistic bone in his body and who couldn't be a worst soulmate for a free-thinking spirit such as yourself?'

'Hold on a minute, you've lost me.' Posy replaced her cup in its saucer. 'Why should it matter whether or not I like the idea?'

'I thought maybe you'd like to join me in my new project?'

'As in, soulmates together in this coach house?' Posy asked her question carefully.

'I was thinking of married soulmates.'

'You're talking nonsense.' Posy gasped.

'I know,' Sam agreed, 'but I'm not sure what I would have done if it had been you who had fallen over the cliff that night. Until that moment I hadn't realised how empty life would without you.'

'You don't know what you're saying,' Posy cautioned.

'You're right. I don't, but when you're in love you say crazy things.'

'You can't be in love with me.'

'Mad, isn't it? The moment you walked into the police station I knew you'd be trouble and I wasn't wrong, was I?'

'What made you change your mind?'

'When that Barry person finally reappeared, looking so smug, I wanted to take a slug at him.

'Then when the whole business started up again with Iris I did wonder if it was another wild goose chase. It didn't take me long to realise I was wrong.'

'About what?'

'Everything, but mainly you. You're tough and resilient and loyal to your friends. You don't care who you upset if you feel your cause is right.'

Posy's ears burned with embarrassment.

'When I realised you weren't the one who had fallen off that cliff I knew I had to tell you how I feel.'

Sam took a deep breath.

'Right, I've had my say. It's your turn. Do I need ear defenders?' he joked.

'There's a table between us. If it wasn't there,' Posy said slowly, 'I might be tempted to take action.'

Sam flattened himself against the back of his seat.

'There's no need to get physical.'

'I'm talking about kissing you.'

A look of amazement replaced Sam's nervous smile.

'Do you? I mean, are you . . . '

'If you're going to be boringly

conventional then, yes, I do love you and yes, I will marry you even though you haven't yet asked me.

'Now about this cottage, when am I going to see it?'

Posy stopped talking as a look of dismay crossed Sam's face.

'What's the matter?' she asked, fearing he might have come to his senses and realised that getting involved with her really was a step too far. 'You've gone pale.'

'I suppose you wouldn't like to try and squeeze round this side of the table would you and sit next to me?'

'Whatever for?'

'Because we could have that kiss you were talking about if you squeeze in close enough and we won't be seen by the rest of the room.'

'It wouldn't be right. You work here.'

'Would it help change your mind if I tell you that your mother, Dulcie and Milo have just come into the lounge?'

'What?'

'Don't turn round. They're looking

for somewhere to sit and if you don't move they'll spot you and come over and join us.'

'I feel like a teenager on a first date!' Posy, having moved with the speed of lightning, snuggled up to Sam. 'Hiding away from the family's prying eyes.'

'In that case, let's not waste any more time,' Sam said.

'Look!' Vera pointed to the alcove. 'Isn't that Posy?'

Milo gestured frantically to Dulcie to do something.

'Why don't we sit over here?' Dulcie tried to guide Vera towards an empty table.

'Who's that she's with?' Vera demanded.

'I'm not sure.' Milo tried to block her view but Vera pushed him to one side.

'It's that very rude man who manhandled Posy away from the exhibition. I'm going to have a word with him.'

'No, you're not.'

'Milo, out of my way.'

'Vera.' Dulcie spoke firmly. 'Will you

please sit down and leave Posy alone?'

'That man's kissing her. How dare he take liberties with my daughter? Milo, can't you do something?'

'I could follow Sam's example,' Milo said, scooping a laughing Dulcie up in his arms.

'For goodness' sake, Milo, everyone's looking at you.'

'Since when has being the centre of attention bothered you, Vera?'

'Is that an engagement ring you're wearing?' Vera spied the ring on Dulcie's finger.

'Do you like it?' Dulcie asked.

'Has everyone in the family gone mad?' Vera demanded.

'It's no good.' Sam released Posy. 'They've seen us.'

'Sorry, Posy.' Milo approached their table hand in hand with Dulcie. 'My diversion tactic didn't work.'

'Yes, it did,' Dulcie replied. 'Look, Vera's ordering a bottle of champagne.'

Posy pushed the tea things to one side.

'In that case, bring it on and we'll have a double celebration.'

'Do you think we're doing the right thing?' Sam asked Dulcie. 'Marrying these twins?'

'Of course you are.' Vera had appeared. 'But don't think for one moment that either of you will be in for a quiet life.'

'I was afraid you'd say something like that,' Sam acknowledged.

There was a soft hiss in the background as the waiter uncorked the champagne.

FESTIVAL FEVER
LOVE WILL FIND A WAY
HUNGRY FOR LOVE
ISLAND MAGIC